PREFACE

As a child of the 1960s, I'm fortunate to remember the older generation of the time, especially my neighbours and family, who could recall the First World War. My grandmother was a young teenager when it ended in 1918. There were neighbours who remembered the war as young adults, many of whom took part in the conflict. They usually reminisced about odd things, like women doing manual labour in factories or other unusual jobs of that time.

My grandfather (on my mother's side) passed away a few months before I was born. Nan remarried a man who we all called Uncle Jack. He was born in 1898. He was also in the trenches during World War One.

Most middle-aged people in the 1960s fought in the Second World War, and there were so many of them. They all had stories to tell, but some of the earlier World War One veterans did not seem so vocal about their times. Or at least, that's how it appeared to me.

Uncle Jack (my step-grandfather) was a very polite man. He had a glass eye, and I always wondered if he had lost it during the Great War. I knew he experienced the trenches, and like all little boys, I wanted to know what it was like. However, something inside stopped me from asking for many years. Then one day, I accompanied him to the off-licence when my mother went to see my grandmother. Uncle Jack and I were walking along the street and I asked him about the Great War. I was about eleven years old at the time. He gave me a few old hardback fiction books inside their postal box covers. I still have them to this day. They were about the Great War and the Boer War and were written in the 1930s.

I suppose I was expecting Uncle Jack to tell me about the trenches, but instead he spoke about the army barracks where he was trained before setting off to the front. He told me about a Welsh sergeant who was full of bluster and discipline. Uncle Jack said this man filled everyone with great dread. It was apparent that the entire unit or squad felt nervous during the morning inspections.

On my walk from Nan's house to the off-licence, I got a run-down on how to make sure a soldier spit and polished his boots to an exceptional degree, so that the toecaps on the army boots looked like mirrors.

I never pressed Uncle Jack further on the subject of the Great War and I never found out how he lost his eye.

However, many years later, I met another World War One veteran. An old man we called Pop. He told me a little more about his experience. This chat was back in 1982 when I was twenty-one. Pop was my first wife's grandfather, and I was sitting with him as he reminisced. We had just been introduced, and I was in his living room, looking up at a photograph of young Pop in his Royal Navy uniform of 1918. He was with his late wife on their wedding day. He said that just after the photo was taken, he was injured aboard a ship in an offshore coastal bombardment near Belgium. He lost much of his hearing. His friends lay around him in bits. Pop told me that it was a ghastly sight and one he would never forget. He hadn't long been married and feared he would never get home to his wife. Fortunately, he did return to his Norfolk town of Gorleston. Pop lived to be ninety.

THE RED BARON'S SKY

C. A. Powell

VISITING HIS GREAT GRANDAD

Philip Armitage turned off the car radio just as the rock artist Siouxsie and the Banshees' latest single 'Happy House' was fading to an end. He thought to let the song run the course, knowing Ronnie would be listening to it. He glanced at his son on the back seat via his rear-view mirror, smiled then turned his attention to the last section of the lane he was driving the Cortina Mark IV along. Bungalows on one side with open fields on the other.

'Dad, how old is Great Grandad today?' asked young Ronnie. He was looking down at his crimson plastic model triplane of the Fokker DR1. It was completely built and painted by his father with all the German decals and looked very realistic, in the youngster's opinion.

'Great Grandad is eighty-two today, Ronnie. He was born in 1898 when Queen Victoria was still alive.' His dad smiled at him via the rear-view mirror.

'Did you really get a card with a number badge for that age?' Ronnie giggled.

'I certainly did. In that old hardware store. The man does bespoke badges.' Philip laughed.

'What's bespoke?' Ronnie asked.

'Something special for a certain thing or occasion. Grandad is very old and birthday card shops don't do age badges for grown-ups.'

'I know.' Ronnie smiled. 'I think they stop at about seven.'

'Is that so?' Philip laughed at his son's knowledge. 'So why is that then, Ronnie?'

'Because I know I'll be seven next birthday and I'll have grown out of age badges by then.' Ronnie suddenly had a matter-of-fact attitude about the whole thing concerning birthday badges.

'So how do you think Pop will react to a birthday badge with eighty-two on it?' Philip said, chuckling.

'I think Pop will laugh,' Ronnie replied. 'After all, Nan said Pop would. Nan told Mum this the other day. And Nan is Pop's daughter. Nan is old and Pop can remember when Nan was a little baby.'

'That's a long time ago.' Philip laughed, humouring his son.

'Does Pop remember Queen Victoria then?' asked young Ronnie inquisitively.

His father chuckled. 'Of course not. I think he was only about two when the old queen died. He would have been six years old by April 1904. The same age you are now.'

'Was he living in Ireland back then?' asked Ronnie.

'Of course,' laughed his father, 'Great Grandaddy is Irish and from Dublin.'

'In school we learned that Queen Victoria died in 1901. If Grandad was born in 1898, he would have been three then.' Ronnie was good at maths. At least, he believed he was.

'Well, Great Grandad wouldn't have been three until the 5th April 1901, Ronnie. As you know it's the 5th April today. That means he was still two when the old queen died in January 1901. Did they teach you the months at school too?' His father laughed again as he changed gears and indicated to turn right into the drive of a suburban bungalow.

'No, they didn't,' replied Ronnie. 'But Great Grandad would have been two and a half. Not two.'

His father stopped the car on the drive's stone shingle. He laughed while pulling up the handbrake and switching off the ignition. 'Alright then, big stuff. We'll settle for two and a half years.'

Ronnie smiled and decided it was an acceptable compromise. 'Alright then.'

The young lad watched as his father got out of the car then opened his rear passenger door. He had already unlocked his seat belt.

'Hello, Nanny,' he called when his grandmother opened the kitchen side door by the drive.

'Hello, Ronnie,' she replied with a delighted smile.

'It's Pop's birthday today, isn't it?' he said excitedly. All the children referred to Great Grandad as Pop.

'It is indeed, Ronnie. Pop is eighty-two today. With you at one end and Pop at the other, there are four generations of us today.'

'Eighty-two is very old, Nanny. Is he in the living room on his favourite armchair?'

'He is,' she replied.

'Did he get his birthday letter from New Zealand?' Ronnie enquired. His great grandfather always got a letter from New Zealand before his birthday.

His grandmother smiled. 'He has indeed, Ronnie. Pop always gets a letter from New Zealand just before his birthday. The New Zealand letter always turns up without fail and always a few days before Pop's birthday. Ever since I was a little girl.' She laughed.

'Has he opened and read it?' Ronnie grinned.

'Not yet, Ronnie. It's a bit of a ritual with Pop. He gets the letter a few days before his birthday and waits until the very day of his birthday before opening it. Usually after his dinner. Then in the evening, he will sit at the table and write a letter back to his friend in New Zealand. He has always done this. As I have already said, ever since I could remember as a little girl. I was no older than you when I first saw him writing back to his friend in New Zealand.'

'That's a very long time, Nanny,' Ronnie replied.

His grandmother chuckled. 'Why not go in and wish him a happy birthday?'

'Yes, I shall.' Ronnie looked excited and was about to enter the house.

'Don't forget your birthday card, Ronnie,' his dad added. He gave the lad his card then bent forward and kissed his mother-in-law on the cheek. 'Are you alright, Mum?'

'I'm well, thank you, Philip,' she replied.

'Is Mum in there with Pop?' asked Ronnie, about to leave them.

'No, your mother has just gone down to the shops with Grandad to run a few errands. She'll be back very shortly. Go on now, Ronnie. Go through to your old Pop. He'll be very pleased to see you.'

Without hesitation, Ronnie entered the house and went to find his great grandfather in the lounge, watching afternoon sports on television.

'Hello, Pop. You are eighty-two today,' Ronnie said with his usual chirpy manner, offering the old man his birthday card. There was a line of other birthday cards along the mantelpiece and to the side was a small round table with a bottle of Irish whiskey on standby next to an empty whiskey glass.

'Is that Pop's lemonade?' asked Ronnie innocently.

Old Pop smiled at his great grandson and replied in his humorous Dublin accent, 'It certainly is, young Ronnie. Purely for medicinal purposes.' He halted and looked at the envelope being offered. 'Why now, would that be for me? So, I'm eighty-two, am I? And there was I, thinking I was just eighteen again.'

'I think you were eighteen a long while ago, Pop,' Ronnie added innocently.

Pop laughed a little more. 'Well now, young Ronnie. You have a fine way of putting things, that's for sure.'

'This is for you, and we got a special card with an eighty-two badge on it. They can make them in the hardware store.'

'Do they really, young Ronnie? Well, would you fancy that.' Old Pop smiled as he opened the envelope and pulled out the card. Sure enough, there was a blue badge with the figures eighty-two upon it.

'I've not seen one that old before,' added Ronnie, as innocent as ever.

Again, Pop chuckled. 'Well, I can honestly say that I've never seen one with a number as high either, Ronnie. And I never expected to...' The old man trailed off and looked down at the plastic plane in Ronnie's hand.

'Are you alright, Pop?' young Ronnie enquired, realising that Pop was interested in his model aeroplane.

'What is that you have there, lad?' The old man leaned forward to look at his assembled and painted model.

Ronnie held up the red plastic German Fokker DR1 model. 'It's a German First World War plane, Pop. My dad made it for me. It has all the painting and the pilot inside. Look! It's the Red Baron. This is a plane the Red Baron had in the First World War.'

'My word, young Ronnie. You gave me a turn looking at that thing, so you did. Jesus, Mary and Joseph! Sixty-two years to the day. My twentieth birthday and this plane. This is a real omen, that's for sure. The Red Baron's plane. Will you let me look at it for a moment, Ronnie?'

'Yes, Pop.' The lad gave his great grandfather the plastic model to scrutinise.

Pop gasped between pursed lips. 'My word, that is awfully close. That red colour and even the white vertical tail fin. Your dad got that part right. The red was a wee bit deeper, as I recall. And the front part was streaked with grease stains. I can remember that part very clearly. The pilot's leather was darker than this little man's here in the cockpit. He also had thick black goggles and just below his throat by the top collar button, hung a Pour le Mérite. His red scarf would normally cover it but the wind in the sky that day blew it back, and I could see the gold gleam and the blue bars of the Red Baron's Blue Max. I always remember that tiny slither of blue cross on top of a circular array of gold. That's how close he got. This little figure doesn't have that fluttering scarf and the Blue Max.'

Ronnie's eyes widened excitedly as his mouth dropped open. 'Did you see the Red Baron in the sky, Pop?'

Pop leaned back in his armchair and nodded as though confused by the memory. 'Today of all days,' he muttered. 'Once again, and on my birthday. That plane is coming back at me through the hazy years. My word, that was a birthday to remember. It shaped my entire life and defined who I am today, young Ronnie.'

Ronnie looked at the plastic model plane that Pop held. The lad's prized World War One Fokker DR1. 'Did you really see this plane, Pop?'

'Oh yes, boy. For sure, I saw this very plane. You never forget the Red Baron's plane. Especially when he's coming for you.' Pop blew at the front of the plastic Fokker DR1 aircraft and watched the propeller spin. He was looking straight at it and blowing every time the propeller slowed down. 'That's what I saw. That's what I kept aiming at. Short bursts. Stop focus as it jostled up and down one side to another. Don't let it settle to shoot us. Pa, pa, pa, pa. Stop aim. Pa, pa, pa. Good Lord, that brings back disturbing memories, young Ronnie, so it does.'

'Did you really see the Red Baron, Pop? Can you tell me about it, Pop? Please, Pop? Can you tell me about it?'

'It was the very same day I met this fella,' said Pop, holding an airmail letter with a New Zealand stamp upon it.

'Is that your birthday letter from your special birthday friend in New Zealand?' Ronnie smiled.

'It is so, young Ronnie. My good old friend Tibby. Since 1924, he has sent me a letter every year on my birthday because we first met on my birthday in 1918.'

'Can you tell me about it, Pop? Is that when you saw the Red Baron, Pop?'

Old Pop laughed and decided his great grandson should know the story of his twentieth birthday back in April 1918. 'It was the first time I met my special friend, Gregory "Tibby" Tibbit.'

As he was about to begin, Philip came into the living room and Ronnie looked up at his father. 'Dad! Pop is going to tell us a true story.'

TIBBIT'S FIRST DAY – APRIL 5TH, 1918

The commotion was over. The unwell cadet, an observer-in-training, was stretchered to the green canvas covering of the Ford Model T field ambulance. The man groaned in agony, but one of the ambulance men spoke reassuringly to him.

'Don't worry, sir, we'll have you at the hospital in no time.'

The breeze surged and the canvas sides swelled. A light ripple ran along the thick fabric and over the big white circle with a central red cross. The stretcher bearers gently slid the groaning observer under the covering and then one climbed in to watch the stricken man.

'Alright, lads, commotion's over,' called the medic from the back of the field ambulance.

11

'Who was it?' asked the new recruit to a fellow standing next to him. The young admin man was about to answer, but another voice responded quicker.

'The newly arrived Officer Cadet Sullivan. Appendix, I think. A young observer-in-training, so I've heard,' the flight sergeant answered without turning to face the new recruit.

'He's only been out on two flights,' said a mechanic.

'Not much luck with observers of late,' mentioned another man close by. He frowned, scrutinising Tibbit in his clean, new beige overalls, complete with the new RAF emblems on the left breast and on his forage cap.

'You've not come over from RNAS, have you?' asked the mechanic.

'No,' replied Tibbit nervously. 'I was RFC, and they gave me this clobber yesterday before arriving here. All the new stuff has RAF now.'

Tibbit looked around at all the fellow mechanics, feeling a little self-conscious. These were the men he would be working with. Many were still wearing RFC forage caps instead of the updated RAF ones. Perhaps they weren't keen on the new amalgamation with the RNAS. There had been rivalry between the two groups.

Another voice called out as they watched the ambulance start up and move away. 'RNAS don't have air mechanics 3rd class.' Tibbit nodded in agreement. He never knew anything about the old RNAS ranks but was happy to acknowledge anything that lent weight to his not being former RNAS.

'I hope they don't start asking for mechanics to volunteer again,' said a mechanic 1st class.

'We're very short on observers,' replied another. 'Especially on a Biff-only airfield like this. One less observer than the number of Biffs. Not a good sign.'

'Biffs?' Tibbit asked, looking the completely naïve recruit.

The flight sergeant in front of Tibbit turned and faced him for the first time. He had a neat, trim moustache and looked the part of a dashing pilot. He still had the old defunct RFC emblem upon his olive-green khaki Maternity tunic. The man smiled politely and answered Tibbit. 'We call our Bristol F2Bs, Biffs. Other aircraft might be called kites, but we call ours affectionately Biffs.'

'Oh,' replied a better-educated Tibbit concerning Bristol F2B aeroplanes. He knew he would be working on such aircraft, having been informed before arrival at the airfield.

'How long have you been here, mate?' asked another mechanic.

'About half an hour,' Tibbit replied. 'I've just left the office.'

The conversation was over. The ambulance was trundling off with the ill observer and the throng of aircraft personnel was dispersing.

'Come on, lads,' yelled a warrant officer as he slowly approached the scattering men. 'Back to your points of duty now. The cadet is in good hands. In a few hours' time Cadet Sullivan will be saying good-bye to his appendix and probably good riddance.'

There were a few chuckles. At least the sick observer would be alright. It had been nothing more than a minor drama.

Air Mechanic 3rd Class Gregory Tibbit turned away from the scene and crossed the wet turf towards the distant aircraft hangar. He was an enthusiastic young recruit with his first duty to attend. A nineteen-year-old that was feeling rather pleased with his new work overalls and forage cap. Once away from the throng, the insecurity he felt vanished. He was apt to being a little vain, liking new and smart-looking things. Once again, he gazed down at his pristine, light brown overalls. Overalls were always clean when first put on from the stores. How long such a condition would last was anyone's guess. He looked at the envelope clasped in his hand. Major Laws had instructed him to deliver the envelope to the mechanic he was reporting to. He also had to pass on a verbal message for a Lieutenant Adams.

This was Tibbit's first responsibility, and he knew he had to handle it with enthusiasm. It was what was expected of him.

'Well, this is it, Tibby old fruit. Our first day of active service on a fully functioning airfield,' he whispered to himself delightedly. He noticed that no one paid him much attention anymore.

The commotion around the ambulance took up most of the observational interest. Yet he was a new face. He expected people to look at him. Apart from the small group during the medical drama, no one else did. It left him feeling a little put out by such a lack of attention. Nothing too elaborate was wanted, but a little scrutiny with a look that said, 'Who is that?' would be welcome while making his lonely walk to the hangar.

Young Air Mechanic 3rd Class Tibbit, with his freshly scrubbed face, sighed to himself. 'Perhaps clean-cut recruits are two a penny at this airfield unit? After all, they've just carted one poor sod off.' He continued walking briskly across the damp turf with a sense of purpose, developing a confident swagger. He passed a group of mechanics – three men lost in their endeavours. All three looking over another Ford Model T truck, though this truck was quite different from the ambulance, and Tibbit couldn't fathom if the servicemen were concerned with the engine or the strange mounted apparatus of the Hucks prop rotator. Not one of the occupied mechanics spared him a glance.

With reluctant acceptance, Tibbit stopped a few feet away from the mechanics and their Hucks truck and observed the approach of a Bristol F2B biplane coming in to land. This was a scene more worthy of his scrutiny.

He frowned. No one seemed to be interested in this either. But then it was an operational airfield and planes must be coming in and taking off on a regular basis.

'Old hat for you lot,' Tibbit muttered to himself concerning the airfield personnel's lack of attention. He would indulge himself and watch the gentle descent of the Bristol F2B aircraft. Listening to the rumbling engine ticking over – feeling the awe as the near forty-foot wingspan of the biplane lowered behind the rotating propeller. The aircraft bounced ever so slightly as the wheels hit the wet grass and then settled into a roll, a trivial wobbling that took the aircraft along the soil. It looked like a perfect landing. The graceful flying machine rolled to a stop just beyond the servicemen working on the Hucks truck, and Tibbit watched the little saga play out. The young observer stood and waved to a few air mechanics coming from one of the tent hangars to greet their returned aircrew.

'Well, I suppose that's that then,' Tibbit whispered as he looked down at himself once again and struck up a conversation with his imaginary sentient overalls. 'At least I have you clean fatigues. You'll not stay clean for long. Not once Tibby starts working on engines, doing armourer duties and welding. Plus, some rigger's work. You'll be all nice and grubby in no time. That'll be a shame.' He stopped and looked about. Thinking to himself was fine, but he should try to stop the progression of turning such thoughts to muttering. It didn't always go down well – talking to oneself.

Another two ground staff were carrying an old wooden door. They never acknowledged the new recruit either. Everyone seemed wrapped up in their own little airfield chores. There was nothing special about an air mechanic 3rd class. Nothing at all.

Yet the slightly put-out Tibbit thought there was always something special about himself. He decided that he didn't need the acknowledgement of others. He looked at the morning dew and enjoyed the gleam of the damp grass. He flattered himself that the sheen of the grass complemented his vibrant fresh look and feel.

The large canvas aircraft hangar, where he was told to report, grew in stature as he progressed towards it. He took another breath of clear morning air and ran his fingers over his fatigues again. His new emblem on his left breast displaying the new RAF letters. As were the letters on his updated forage cap. He reasoned that his new overalls were the first among all of the staff. He had noticed no other RAF badges. They were all wearing the old defunct RFC emblem on their dirty work fatigues.

The Royal Flying Corps had ceased five days ago. As of April Fools' Day, they were now the Royal Air Force. *Perhaps they should have left it a few days,* thought Tibbit.

A tall lean-looking lieutenant came out of the hangar and scrutinised the recruit. The officer put a cigarette to his lips and lit it. Tibbit estimated him to be about twenty-five years old. His close-cut black hair and thin moustache gave him a demeanour of experience and confidence. He looked resplendent in his smart olive-green khaki Maternity tunic with his two shoulder pips. His breeches were sand-coloured, and he wore black knee-length boots. He still wore the defunct RFC emblem of the Royal Flying Corps.

'Well, aren't we a pretty boy then,' said the lieutenant as he noticed Tibbit's RAF emblem on his forage cap and fatigues.

'Yes, sir,' Tibbit replied and saluted sheepishly, thinking that the officer seemed unusually relaxed and familiar among the lower ranks. Still, someone beyond the ambulance commotion had finally noticed him in his upgraded fatigues. Once again, he felt embarrassed and naïve about it.

'Is it your first active tour of duty on this fine spring day?' asked the lieutenant, humorously returning the salute as he drew on his cigarette in the other hand. He then looked up at the clear blue sky. He seemed rather unauthoritative but retained his officer style. A dashing nonchalance for a man of officer rank. Tibbit suspected there was also a touch of nervous fatigue behind the wall of bravado.

'Yes, sir. It's my first day of duty,' Tibbit replied. 'I've been told to give this card to Air Mechanic 1st Class Maloney. And could Lieutenant Adams report to Major Laws as soon as possible.'

'Well, how jolly. A nice cosy little chat with the major. The Lieutenant Adams part is me. I presume you're the new lad, AM 3rd Tibbit?'

'Yes, sir,' Tibbit replied, nervously.

'Don't worry, Tibbit, we don't bite. And AM 1st Maloney is in there working on the foster mounting above my cockpit. I presume the envelope is a birthday card,' said Adams. 'It's Maloney's twentieth birthday today. Major Laws always acknowledges each man's birthday. He seems to have a thing about that.'

'Oh,' Tibbit replied. 'Perhaps it is, sir. It does look like one, now that you mention it.'

'Not sure why Major Laws didn't use that wonderful telephone contraption we have in the office to call me over,' added Adams. 'I smell a little rat of something important. A face-to-face right along the line. I wonder what our Major Laws is after. He could have still summoned me by telephone – he has a direct link from his office to this hangar.'

'Perhaps the major thought I could kill two birds with one stone, sir?' said Tibbit. 'I'm coming here and might as well pass a message on?'

Lieutenant Adams chuckled and took another draw on his cigarette then dropped it and ground it out in the soil. 'You'll find Major Laws always has a reason for such an approach. Something he wants kept under wraps, no doubt. He doesn't like using the telephone unless he has to. That's usually when the real bigwigs ring in.'

'Oh,' was all Tibbit could say.

Both men stopped and watched a large French truck slowly pass by the tent opening. Lieutenant Adams smiled at the two French soldiers inside the driving cabin covered with another crude canvas covering.

Adams chuckled as the two French soldiers grinned approvingly. They knew exactly what the British airman laughed at. The passenger stood and saluted, then called out, 'N'est-ce pas mieux, Lieutenant?' The driver remained smiling but intent on the steering wheel and edged the big truck over the turf towards another tent hangar.

Adams called back jovially, 'C'est une belle amélioration, Caporal Charpentier.'

As the De Dion-Bouton truck chugged by, the young French corporal bowed good-humouredly before the canvas covering obscured him from view while Tibbit looked at the big white number seven grinning through the smeared mud upon the green wood panelling.

'What are French personnel doing here, sir?' Tibbit was intrigued.

'Oh, just some swops, old boy. Sometimes the French have a surplus of things from the kitchens and sometimes we have a surplus of different things. We swop whenever we can. The last time, our French friends had an open top and got drenched in a downpour of rain.'

'Oh, so that's what that bit of banter was about, the canvas covering, sir?'

'It certainly was, old boy. Whenever you see that Froggie De Dion-Bouton truck with the seven grinning through the mud, you know it's the swopsy chaps. They come over from the French airfield a little way south. The French are often after our Bisto gravy granules, among other things. They seem to like the browning and seasoning together.'

'Oh,' Tibbit replied as he watched the truck stop before a long tent hangar. 'Is that the cook house where the truck has stopped?'

Adams smiled. 'It is, AM Tibbit. However, you'll find our Maloney inside here. He's the Irish lad. I'll see what Major Laws wants.' He then headed towards the wooden office complex from where Tibbit had just walked over.

Tibbit watched the officer saunter off for a few seconds before turning to the open hangar. He was eager about getting to work on any aircraft the top brass might bring before him. And so he entered the big tent hangar, ready to dispatch the birthday card to Air Mechanic 1st Class Maloney. The very man he was instructed to report to for his work roster.

He looked delightedly at the two Bristol F2B biplanes inside, noting the grey-painted top section of the engine casing. And, what appeared to be, a bronze hooped strip that ran around the front section. It separated the front air grid partition from the grey cowling. The front vents were closed, hiding the rotary engine cylinders. Beneath, beyond the grey front, ran the sand-coloured under panel. This light-sand paint also ran along the underneath of the wings. Why this sandy khaki was underneath was beyond him. He thought it might have been a sky-blue colour. Apart from the grey forward top section of the engine cowling, the rest of the plane was an olive-green khaki like most of the planes' canvas coverings. He scrutinised the fabric rack tool by a work bench – he had used this device at the training school. He looked back at one of the Bristol F2Bs and noted how well the thick rib lacing was done, crisscrossing along rivets on the frame and ring holes in the blanket-laid fabric – like thick, tidy, pristine shoelaces.

'Overlapping canvas layers applied blanket method,' he whispered to himself delightedly. All the bindings pulled the overlapping canvas against the metal frames. Although it appeared basic, Tibbit understood the art of the application and additions too. Then he winced as he imagined bullets ripping through such coverings with ease when flying in the windswept blue sky. Yet despite such vulnerability, there was something artistic and beautiful about the grand machine of the air.

Each elegant-looking flying vehicle was being worked on by dedicated young air mechanics. Tibbit's eyes ran along the aircraft again, examining the flying wires and the inner struts keeping the wings secure and the right distance apart. So much intricate wiring. So many small things that could go wrong. He envisaged a pyramid of playing cards collapsing and dismissed the thought quickly.

Tibbit took a deep breath and reminded himself, with satisfaction, 'This will be my workspace for some time to come.'

Two maintenance crew looked over one aircraft's dark varnished propeller. The other aircraft had a single maintenance man in very greasy buff overalls standing at the top of a small ladder. He was fiddling about with the foster mounting above the pilot's empty cockpit. On the lower port wing beside the lone mechanic sat a big tabby tom cat, watching the worker – a man that cussed and cursed as he removed the front upper central wing's Lewis machine gun from the mounting. Just behind the pilot's seat was a second, rear cockpit. A place for an observer to sit. Below the opening and along the side canvas was writing – big block capital letters below the rim that read: THIS MACHINE MUST NOT BE FLOWN WITHOUT PASSENGER OR EQUIPMENT WEIGHT IN GUNNER'S COCKPIT.

'Next will be the blooming foster mounting, so it will,' hissed Air Mechanic Maloney to the old tom cat in a Dublin accent. He climbed down from the ladder with the Lewis gun and walked to a table with the weapon. He placed it on a work bench beside an old, outdated copy of *The War Illustrated* – a bright red circle with 2d weekly written inside the scarlet circumference. Maloney was about to return to the plane but checked himself. Tibbit was standing before the air mechanic's scrutiny. A fresh recruit in his clean new overalls and his new RAF badge and RAF forage cap.

Maloney grinned. He was still wearing his old RFC forage cap. 'Don't tell me now! You're the new AM three – Tibbit. I've been told to expect you. What you got there, a birthday card from Major Laws? That'll be for me, no doubt.'

'I think so. Lieutenant Adams said as much. He's going to see Major Laws now.'

'Oh, is he really? I never heard the telephone ring,' said Maloney, accepting the envelope with a grin.

'The major didn't call on the telephone,' Tibbit replied. 'He asked me to pass the message on to Lieutenant Adams personally.

The lieutenant was also surprised there was no telephone call.'

'Well now, that is strange.' Maloney frowned. 'I wonder what that's about. A sit-down in the major's office. Probably a cup of tea and a digestive biscuit. It means that Lieutenant Adams and his observer are being briefed on some sort of mission. A reconnaissance one, I would bet. You'll be helping me assemble a small camera crate by the rear cockpit after we take down the foster mounting. This photo crate is one of our own designs. If it were up to me, I'd just hold the blooming camera.' He grinned as he ripped open the envelope. Maloney hissed in mock delight as he pulled out a birthday card with a coloured sketch of a Bristol F2B aircraft.

Tibbit was looking about the work area. There was an old advert behind the work bench. It was stuck to the metal door of a store unit – a patriotic poster, and Tibbit wondered if it was now an image of sarcasm and ridicule among the mechanics. It was a cartoon diagram of two planes. One British and one German. Above the two planes were the words in block capital letters: JOIN THE ROYAL AIR FORCE AND SHARE IN THEIR HONOUR AND GLORY.

Below the image of the two planes and in a gold-rimmed frame was written: Age 18 to 50. RATES OF PAY from 1/6 to 12/- per day.

Then below that was writing in smaller letters: (If you join the Royal Air Force voluntarily, you cannot be transferred to the Army or Navy without your own consent.)

Maloney was reading his birthday card. 'Well now, isn't that kind of our Major Laws? That makes me feel all warm and wanted, so it does.' He sniggered and looked over to the other plane where the two mechanics were still inspecting the propeller. He waved his card at them.

One of the mechanics noticed and called back good-humouredly, 'Oh, my word! Our Maloney has got himself a birthday card. Getting in the major's good books, are we?'

The second mechanic looked back and grinned. 'Are we going to get a slice of cake?'

Maloney turned to his new recruit and helper, Tibbit. 'Did yer hear that, Tibby? You must get called Tibby? All our Norris and Cooper want is blooming cake. Can you imagine that?'

Tibbit smiled and realised the maintenance crew was a light-hearted bunch of men. 'Well, I suppose it makes sense for your birthday. Does Major Laws provide cake too?'

An eruption of combined laughter came from Maloney, Norris and Cooper. A gathering of well-intentioned mirth.

'I should be so blooming lucky,' Maloney laughed, 'I have to get such things myself, so I do.'

'The major doesn't like to push the boat out too far,' Norris responded as he and Cooper went back to work on their propeller.

'Well, thanks for bringing the card, Tibby. It is Tibby, isn't it?'

Tibbit smiled. 'Yes, Tibby is always the name my mates adopted. Even back at school and the training ground. It's a good nickname and I like wearing it.'

Maloney grinned. 'Tibby, you are most definitely a fella of quality. If you like and can take a joke as well as the next man, you should fit in nicely here.' He looked back at Norris and Cooper and called out, 'By the way, you fellas, this is AM Three – Gregory "Tibby" Tibbit.'

'Welcome to the nut hutch, Tibby,' called Norris jovially.

'Don't need to be nuts to work here but if you are, it helps,' added Cooper.

Maloney chuckled along with them while Tibbit relaxed a bit. The mechanics were, indeed, very sound men.

'Well, Tibby. You may as well get your hands and new overalls dirtied up.' Maloney selected a couple of spanners and handed them to Tibbit. 'You get up the ladder and stand in the front cockpit. I'll be on the ladder, and we'll have that foster mount off in no time.'

Tibbit took the spanners, and clambered up the ladder and into the front cockpit. Careful not to knock the spoon-shaped grip on the aluminium working stick, he noted the trigger pad inside the triangular grip. Maloney had followed and stopped at the top of the ladder.

'Take a good look, Tibby.' Maloney chuckled. 'I'm presuming you have seen such things at the training ground?'

'Not one of these,' replied Tibbit with a touch of excitement, looking at the closed petrol-adjustment lever next to the downward arrow sign that read: OFF. His eyes quickly searched the wooden control panel and perceived the various clocks and dials – the circular glass container with the compass lying flat within the glass cover, and the air speed clock face starting at 40 mph, going up in 10 mph increments from 50 to 60 to 70, and so on.

'This front panel is a little more involved than the old kite we were learning on back at the training ground. We had a look around a Sopwith Camel on a few occasions. That was a rare old treat. But that didn't have the dials and instruments that this kite has.'

'That's our Biff for you, Tibby. She's easy enough once you've worked on her a few times,' Maloney replied. 'Personally, I like the old Sopwith Camel and the SE5a too.'

'I think I can guess why the pilot might not want the added responsibility of the Lewis above him on the foster mountings,' said Tibbit, looking down at the forward Vickers machine gun. He knew it was synchronised to fire .303 bullets between the propellers. 'I see the Vickers is mounted to the underneath of the cowling. Why is that?'

'Helps prevent the gun from freezing,' Maloney replied.

Tibbit nodded. It made sense as to why the upper front-firing Lewis gun had been taken down. 'Did the pilot have to stand to fire the Lewis on the top wing?'

'You got it, Tibby. An unnecessary thing for some pilots. Doesn't help the compass much either. The Vickers alone is a nice bit of kit at the pilot's fingertips. Look at the thumb pad inside the spad grip. You still have to point the plane at the target to hit anything, however. Some pilots like the extra Lewis on its foster mountings – you get a wider range of fire all round – but it can also be a big distraction from other duties for the pilot. It depends on the individual. Lieutenant Adams can't get on with it and has requested for it to be removed. The rear cockpit observer has another Lewis gun for aircraft approaching from behind. This rear gun has a wide angle of fire with the swing gun, or the Scarff mount as we call it. The rachet teeth give the gun a nice lift too.'

'Yes, I noticed that,' added Tibbit. 'I thought the rear gunners had double Lewis guns?'

'Again, some crews do. But double Lewis guns are a little more cumbersome to manoeuvre on their mounts at high altitude. Especially up and down with the rachet teeth you see at the side of the mount. Many prefer a single Lewis gun at the rear. Easier to swivel about. Again – it depends on the observer's preference, so it does.'

'That makes sense. A double Lewis gun would be a little more difficult to move about even on mounts,' Tibbit agreed.

'Have you used the Lewis, Tibby?' asked Maloney.

'Only at the training grounds. The short burst, halt and aim again for another three or four short bursts. They seemed very insistent about the short bursts.'

'Allows for the coolant vents to stop the barrel from overheating.'

Tibbit began to loosen the fastenings of the curved Lewis gun mount at the centre of the top of the upper wing.

Within moments, both men were using spanners to disengage the foster mounting frame away from the central upper wingspan. The small rail fixture came away easily. Gingerly, Tibbit helped as Maloney slowly descended the ladder holding his rungs of the frame while Tibbit kept his grip above, waiting for the senior mechanic to reach the ground. The whole disassembling had taken a few minutes of nut and bolt loosening.

'Right ho, Tibby. Let her go. I've got her.'

Tibbit complied and scrambled out of the cockpit and down the rungs while Maloney placed the frame next to the Lewis gun on the work bench.

Cooper called over, 'Oi, Dermot. When are you leaving Lieutenant Adams' Biff for tea?'

Maloney smiled and replied, 'Well now, Tibby and I'll put these parts in the stores and then get a quick brew going.' He looked back at Tibbit. 'Lucky you, Tibby. A tea break and birthday cake after your first ten minutes of work. We'll store these parts and then have some tea and cake before attaching the camera equipment by the side of the rear cockpit for our observer. Cadet Sullivan likes it on the starboard side. The other observers preferred the port side. We cater for each aircrew's personal preferences and the crate design can easily be taken from one side to another. I'm constantly saying, if I were an observer, I would just hold the blooming camera against the fuselage, take the picture and return to the cockpit for a slide change when needed.'

Tibbit followed Maloney across the hangar to the small counter holding the Lewis gun. He placed it on the wooden top beside the mountings that Maloney had put down. The senior mechanic went about the task of storing the items in their relevant areas. Tibbit's interest was caught by the nine cylinders of a Clerget rotary engine lying upon another sturdy work bench close by. It was very dirty with oil all over its nine cylinders.

'These rocker arms look like they've seen better days,' Tibbit said.

'The whole blooming thing needs taking apart and a complete overhaul,' muttered Maloney with an edge to his voice.

'You don't put Clergets into these kites, do you?'

Maloney laughed. 'No, Tibby. We don't do things like that now.'

'You've had a Sopwith Camel in here then?' Tibbit raised an enquiring eyebrow.

'Very good, Tibby. Ten house points for you. We spent some time on that kite. Changing the entire rotary engine for a new one. First flight out and the pilot got shot down – the poor sod.'

Tibbit was shocked. 'Sorry, I wasn't meaning to be—'

'Oh, don't be feeling bad about it, Tibby. You'll see these things happening about us all of the time. You'll meet a few pilots that you like. These fellas come and go, so they do. Most of them actually. Try not to get too attached to the airmen. Always be friendly but be aware. Many won't be around for long.'

'I'll bear that in mind.' Tibbit frowned.

'Anyways…' began Maloney. 'Let's get a brew going, shall we?'

He beckoned Tibbit to follow him to a small coal-fired stove with a large kettle upon it.

After some thought, Tibbit asked, 'Did you say Cadet Sullivan liked the camera in such a way?'

'Yes, Cadet Sullivan is Lieutenant Adams' new observer. He came along three days ago.'

Tibbit rubbed the back of his neck and continued, 'Without meaning to sound disrespectful, but a cadet observer-in-training was carted off in an ambulance about twenty minutes ago. It was on the other side of those huts.' He pointed to the distant pavilion. 'The ambulance would have been hidden by the complex from here. Therefore, you wouldn't have noticed the commotion. The cadet observer was called Sullivan. They think he has something wrong with his appendix.'

Maloney looked back with open-mouthed surprise and replied, 'Oh bejesus! Not Sullivan! Not another observer?' He put on some thick gloves and took the hot kettle off the stove and poured a smidgeon of hot water into the empty teapot. He placed the big kettle back on the stove and took a tin box of tea leaves from the shelf. Then he swirled the hot water about the teapot before slinging the contents onto the sod. Maloney was silent as he put a few spoonfuls of tea leaves into the heated teapot, then once again picked up the simmering kettle and poured more hot water into the teapot and stirred it with a big wooden ladle.

'Are we low on observers then?' asked Tibbit.

'We are indeed, Tibby. And take a bit of advice from me...' 'Right ho,' Tibbit agreed as he watched Maloney, waiting for his own acknowledgement. The senior mechanic continued stirring the tea leaves in the hot teapot with a concerned look on his face.

'Don't volunteer to learn anything outside of your mechanical duties. Rigging, armouring, welding and engine mechanics are fine. Don't volunteer for map-reading, photography or anything outside of your groundwork duties. Trust me, it'll come around and bite you on the flaming backside, so it will.' He looked over to Norris and Cooper and called, 'Tea up!'

The sound of metal tools being placed on work benches clanged across the hangar and Norris and Cooper came over to the stove. Maloney pulled out a brown paper bag from a small cupboard close by. He also brought out a spare tin cup.

'You may as well use this cup, Tibby.' 'Thanks,' he replied.

Norris and Cooper were both six feet tall. Norris was heavy-set with a big, hooked nose and square chin, while Cooper was very thin with a small nose and a weak chin above a huge Adam's apple. Each man's face was covered in sweat and oil streaks.

Maloney sniggered. 'Will you be looking at these two, Tibby. It's obvious these fellas have been wiping sweat off their faces without clean rags.'

'I would guess with the cuffs of their oil-soaked sleeves,' said Tibbit, laughing.

The two mechanics arrived at the stove and unfolded canvas chairs to sit on. Maloney got out two fold-up wooden chairs and gave one to Tibbit. 'There you go, Tibby, have a seat.'

Tibbit sat down and looked at the cheerful expectant faces of Norris and Cooper, slightly oil-smeared, yet comical, happy men nonetheless.

Then came the sound of rustling brown paper as Maloney unwrapped the bag and began to cut sections of the carrot cake.

'Where did you get that?' asked Cooper with an admiring smile.

'Did a deal with the cook house,' replied Maloney. His mood was suddenly sombre as he concentrated on his task. 'The old Froggie swop truck had been in. Got some ingredients in exchange for those gravy granules they're always after. The cook knocked this up for me.'

'What did the cook want in return?' asked Cooper.

'Just some tobacco,' replied Maloney in a subdued matter-of-fact manner.

Norris raised an enquiring eyebrow. 'What's wrong, Dermot? You look like you've lost a shilling and found a threepenny bit.'

'Well there, fella, I think I've got a wee problem, so I have,' he replied. 'Our Tibby saw a cadet observer-in-training carted away on a stretcher. The fella was loaded aboard an ambulance, just before our Tibby got here. A very short time ago. It sounds like a dodgy appendix and the young observer's name is Sullivan.' There followed a momentary stunned silence from Norris and Cooper. Each man looked to one another before turning back to Maloney, both with concerned frowns.

'Blooming heck,' gasped Norris. He looked about, making sure no one of rank was in earshot. 'They're short of observers and you learned all that flaming map-reading and photography. What on earth are you going to do? Major Laws has been at this airfield for two weeks now. He never stays this long before moving on to inspect another place. If anyone can make a mad decision, that old fruit cake can.'

'I know,' Maloney agreed as he looked up from cutting the cake. 'This worry wouldn't bother me normally – the old major would be off galivanting about on his usual tour of airfields. All this couldn't have happened at a worse time. If Captain Polden was in charge with Major Laws nowhere in sight, this dilemma would be handled in a different way. But the major is here, and we know he's one for taking the bull by the horns when sorting out a problem, that's for sure.'

Norris gritted his teeth and hissed, 'So you believe that the major will select you as an acting observer-in-training now? The top brass have been taking air mechanics up for a while on other airfields.'

'Only when Major Laws visits,' added Copper.

Young Tibbit looked shocked. 'What's wrong with going up?

Don't you want a chance to do that?'

'No!' the mechanics replied in unison with an emphatic and almost angry tone.

Maloney took a deep breath and held a hand up to his old friends before gently replying to Tibbit. 'The rate of casualties among airmen is rather disturbing, to say the least, Tibby.'

'That's putting it very mildly indeed,' said Norris.

Maloney continued, 'Most of the pilots whose kites we've worked on, the very men we've worked with, are dead. Large numbers of these poor sods don't last. When shot down, it's rare to survive the crash. Did you not know of this, Tibby? Surely you must know?'

Norris looked at Tibbit and added, 'Why do you think the top brass are recruiting from among the lower ranks for flight missions nowadays? Especially where observers are concerned. If they can teach you how to operate a wireless, read maps and use a camera, you can be an acting observer-in-training.'

Cooper continued, 'One such observer taught Dermot about photography. A likeable bloke too. Cadet Observer Brett, that was his name. This observer realised that our Dermot was interested in cameras and photographs. In his spare time, our young Brett helped Dermot as a favour – taught him all about the camera and how to get the best photographs. Then one day, that particular observer and his pilot were shot down. It was some months back. Before going down in flames, our kindly young observer let the major know what an aptitude for photography our Dermot Maloney has. Told the major our Maloney was a complete natural. As one might imagine, very high praise indeed.

'Then, to cap it all, our Maloney was persuaded to look at the other skills on offer. Various topics of interest to stop those odd moments of boredom creeping in. Unfortunately, under the encouragement of "get that one under your belt mate", our Air Mechanic 1st Class Maloney learnt map-reading and Morse code wireless-operating. Now he's just ripe for the picking. Not quite trained the way the top brass want, and not from the right background. However, a trained man nonetheless. One that can be used if necessary. With this form of use comes the seasoned experience of flying as a proper qualified observer.'

'If you can live long enough to become seasoned,' added Norris sarcastically.

Maloney was also annoyed by Cooper and Norris. 'You two are a real bag of giggles, aren't you now? I've not volunteered to go up and I haven't put my name forward.'

Norris swigged his tea, then said, 'But we've noticed that Lieutenant Adams has been called for a brief chat with Major Laws. And we now know that Cadet Observer Sullivan is going for a rather long lie-in. How long do you get off for whipping out a bloke's appendix? I reckon it's a fortnight, especially among young officer ratings. Our Sullivan was meant to go out today. All other qualified observers are assigned to their own duties. If the powers that be are desperate enough, you know they won't mind cutting a corner. And I bet that's the reason Major Laws didn't call on our office telephone. I'm sorry, Maloney, but this isn't good.'

'God love us, Norris. Do you not think I'm aware of this? I just wish you lads would let it be.'

Tibbit could see the air mechanics' concern and was surprised. Then he asked, 'But surely you have to go up a few times before they can make you a qualified observer?'

Maloney looked at Tibbit and added, 'Keep your feet on the ground and stick to the mechanics. So, help me – by the time I realised I was becoming adept and fattened for the kill, it was too late. I thought my lack of flying experience would make me unsuitable. But then, some pilots come here with mere hours under their belts. These are fledgling pilots, mind, and they have to take a kite up by themselves. What chance does a fledgling observer have who already has an experienced pilot to take the kite up?'

'The top brass would waiver that and allow the trained pilot to fly?' Tibbit added tentatively.

'That's right, Tibby. So, we'll guess that my lack of flying know-how will matter for nothing, that's for sure. I can get that experience and knowledge from the pilot on a training flight or with a pilot on a proper mission. What would it matter? If the top brass want me sitting in an observer cockpit taking photographs, they'll have me one way or another.

I have photography, wireless, clock code and map-reading under my belt. The old saying "never volunteer for anything" remains so. I thought I would learn something useful, so I did. A little learning in my spare time. Now I'm thinking something's coming around to bite me on the backside. Lord love us!'

'I thought they would send you away for some months. To train as an observer,' said Tibbit in disbelief.

Maloney sighed before prattling on. He seemed desperate to get things off his chest. 'Usually, they do. It started off as only officers in the aircraft at the start of all this caper. And trust me, these fellas were more than welcome to it. But that changed as the war progressed. I've heard of other mechanics becoming observers, going up after learning such things on the airfield the way I did. And the flying part comes as the acting observer-in-training gets air experience on real missions. After all, I'll be with a qualified pilot, so I will. If that isn't enough flight experience for an acting observer-in-training, I don't know what is. I only need to do the things on which I've been trained. Tasks I'm certain I can now do. Things the top brass know I can now do. Photographing, clock-targeting and Morse code-sending.'

'And our Dermot doesn't need a pilot's licence for that,' added Norris.

'You're a real bucket of laughs, you are, Norris.' Cooper scowled then sipped his hot tea.

'Oh, 'ark at me!' Norris hit back. Cooper was the most vocal concerning Maloney's worrying matter.

'Perhaps it won't come to this.' Tibbit was trying to look on the bright side. He never realised how undesirable flying an aircraft was among the aircraft mechanics, though a short chat on the subject had quickly opened his eyes to the drawbacks and concerns.

Maloney took a deep breath and spoke again. 'I hope you're right, Tibby. I would love it not to come to this. However, I feel this will be one lousy twentieth birthday for me.' He looked at Norris and Cooper. 'I like Lieutenant Adams, but I don't think he'll be here for long. Better pilots have come and gone.'

'That's true,' added Cooper. 'Would have preferred Captain Polden as your pilot.'

Norris nodded. 'That bloke's a survivor. I think he'll get through this. Our young Cadet Observer Elliott will be alright.'

'Yes, thank for that, Norris,' replied Maloney indignantly. 'Norris!' Cooper exclaimed with another scowling look.

'Now what?' Norris was perplexed.

'You're about as subtle as a bucket of sick.' Cooper frowned, shaking his head in disbelief.

'Perhaps Lieutenant Adams is better than we realise,' added Tibbit, hoping to lighten Dermot Maloney's concern. 'He seems like a decent bloke. We can't say what he's like when he's up in the air and far away.'

'You can see what they're like during landing and taking off,' added Norris, hoping he wasn't saying something unsubtle. 'Lieutenant Adams always hangs out with us mechanics, relying too much on our friendship. Underneath his friendly approach, the bloke is nervous. He wants us to like him and give his kite the best possible maintenance. We do that anyway.'

Cooper nodded in agreement and added, 'Lieutenant Adams seems to try too hard to be liked by us lower ranks. That's not a good sign among the officers. They should take a healthy interest, but not become overbearing on the "let's be pals" side of things. Other pilots don't do this type of thing, they usually get sloshed in their officers' mess before the next flight mission. After all, many of the poor sods are on borrowed time and know it.'

'Mind you,' added Maloney, 'Sullivan told me that Lieutenant Adams comes into his own when he's out there. According to our temporarily departed observer, the lieutenant is a climber. Adams loves his Biff's Falcon III Rolls Royce engine. And why wouldn't he? For sure, the man is always going on about how fast he can make his Biff climb. As you know, the Falcon is a lovely engine to work with.'

Tibbit watched all three mechanics nod and murmur approvingly. They all seemed to like working on Rolls Royce aircraft engines.

Cooper nodded again before breaking the brief silence. 'I've heard Adams go on about his Falcon III engine and how smoothly it climbs. He's very lucky to get any Rolls Royce engine at the moment, you know how hard they are to come by. Yet he was lucky enough to get the best Falcon engine going. A blooming mark III to boot. Let's be honest, those things are like gold dust. He can get to ten thousand feet quicker than anyone else in the squadron.'

Maloney cut in, 'And according to Sullivan, he makes splendid use of that advantage.'

'That only stands to reason,' Norris added positively. 'The bloke gets two hundred and seventy-five horsepower from a Falcon III. The Falcon II will only give you two hundred and fifty.'

'But surely the two-fifty is blooming good as well, when you look at some of the engines in the other Biffs.' Cooper took another swig of his tea.

Norris nodded his appreciation. 'Oh of course. All of them are Rolls Royce and reliable, but your Falcon III allowing an extra ten miles per hour will give anyone a faster climb. I suppose it's a good thing the lieutenant is aware of that fact. He clearly appreciates his engine. I'm surprised Captain Polden hasn't tried to commandeer it for his own Biff.'

'What engine does the captain's Biff have?' asked Tibbit tentatively.

All three mechanics stopped and looked at Tibbit, then Maloney replied, 'Our Cooper and Norris are working on Captain Polden's Wolseley Viper engine. A mere one hundred and eighty horsepower.'

Tibbit was visibly shocked. 'That's a big difference between the two planes. Two hundred and seventy-five h.p. against one hundred and eighty. And Captain Polden is the senior officer?'

'The captain loves the Wolseley Viper,' added Norris. 'I think they're unreliable, but the captain seems to get the best out of it.

I don't think he wants the Falcon engine. Never even mentioned it, though I wonder whether he might change his mind if he went up in the lieutenant's Biff.'

'The captain's Wolseley Viper is nothing but constant maintenance,' said Cooper. 'There always seems to be something to tinker with every time the captain returns.'

Maloney swallowed a piece of his cake and then added, 'Oh, I don't think Captain Polden is the sort of man to commandeer Lieutenant Adams' Biff or his Falcon III, even though the engine is much better than the one his own Biff has. It's not the captain's way.'

'I sometimes wonder if the captain has a slight twinge of resentment. Maybe a little envious?' Cooper wondered aloud.

'Especially if Lieutenant Adams goes down with that good engine he has. Might be considered a bit of a waste.'

Maloney hissed, 'Now that's a terrible thing to say, Norris. I'm surprised at you. Maybe the lieutenant needs that added edge and the captain is happy to help his man out. He has lasted longer than expected. Perhaps his Falcon III engine has played a part in this. But for how much longer?'

'So, just to be clear…' Tibbit began. 'You blokes don't think Lieutenant Adams will last long? How can you make these conclusions?'

Norris answered him. 'We pick up on certain things, Tibby. We appreciate how dangerous it is in the RFC. Sorry, my mistake. It's now five days since the RAF was born.'

'Dangerous seems to be the right word from what you lads are saying. I was also led to believe that being an air mechanic was better than being in the trenches or aboard ships, concerning chances of survival?'

'It is, Tibby,' replied Cooper. 'Provided you don't learn things that get you put in an observer's cockpit. Then you're no longer an air mechanic 1st class. Your survival odds tend to drop significantly once you get promoted to Acting Cadet Observer-in-Training. Norris and I have been here for two years. Dermot's been here for just over a year. He was too enthusiastic for his own good. All because of that now departed observer. A recruit who flattered Maloney about his learning abilities. A recruit who taught photography to a lad from the masses, using the very cameras we have here. Then came the Morse code transmitter via another officer and then the compulsory map-reading. Even we had to do that.'

'I deliberately failed it,' replied Norris.

'You failed it because you couldn't learn it,' scolded Cooper. 'Alright,' added Norris. 'That works for me.'

Maloney looked at Tibbit. 'They'll try and get you to learn this too, Tibby. Make sure you display a lack of enthusiasm and aptitude. Or this could happen to you, that's for sure.'

'How are you going to get out of this?' asked Tibbit.

Maloney took a deep breath and looked out of the hangar opening. 'I'm not sure if they'll ask me yet. But if they do, I don't know how I can get out of it. I was full of enthusiasm at first. Then my teachers went out in aircraft and didn't come back. After a while I began to get less enthusiastic, so I did. Lieutenant Adams knows I'm not keen. If Major Laws wants a quiet word about my ability, I hope he gives me a bad recommendation.'

'Would the lieutenant be likely to help you out and do that?' Tibbit sighed. 'You said he wanted to be liked by us lower ranks.'

'When he's in here with us,' Cooper replied.

'When he's with Major Laws, he may want to be liked by the top brass,' Norris concluded.

'It's no good dwelling on things,' added Maloney. 'It might not happen, and we're just speculating. Let's have tea and eat some cake.'

'Happy Birthday, Dermot,' said Norris and Cooper.

'Happy Birthday,' added Tibbit, not sure if he should address the senior mechanic by his first name.

'You can call me Dermot or Maloney, Tibby. Us air mechanics don't stand on ceremony with each other in this hangar.'

'Happy Birthday, Dermot,' he corrected with a smile.

The mechanics reclined as they drank their tea, studying the two Bristol F2B aircraft sat before them awaiting further attention. The light grey engine casing at the front of each aircraft. The six exhaust pipes coming out of the side of the upper casing merged with a longer main exhaust along the side.

'We've got to put an extension on that main exhaust flow so that it goes down and along past Captain Polden's cockpit,' muttered Cooper after sipping his tea.

'Why is that?' asked Tibbit.

Cooper smiled at the recruit. 'The captain says he gets whiffs of exhaust fumes with the end being close to his cockpit. Quite strong when he's still on the ground but reckons he can still get the odd waft when he's up in the sky. Asked for that main exhaust to be longer, running along past the observer cockpit.'

'I notice the exhaust stops within the grey metal casing area,' Tibbit said. 'Would the extension pipe be too close to the green canvas when it's hot?'

'That was suggested to Captain Polden but there are brackets that hold the exhaust away from the canvas plus the wind-rush up there stops it from getting too hot, according to the captain,' added Norris.

Maloney came out of his worried pondering and joined the conversation. 'A couple of the other Biffs have the longer exhaust extensions. I'm of the opinion that a longer pipe could be better, especially if there are fumes.'

Norris looked longingly at his and Cooper's work plane. 'That'll be our next job. Captain Polden asked us to see to it after his return from today's mission. His kite is coming along fine. The propeller timing remains properly in sync with the Vickers gun. The man is a stickler about propeller and gun sync.'

'That sounds rather reasonable to me, Norris.' Maloney giggled and almost choked on his carrot cake. He took a gulp of tea, then added, 'Seeing as how the good captain wouldn't want to shoot his prop off now, would he?'

This last statement was followed by some good-natured chuckling as Cooper shook his head, smiling in disbelief. 'Nice to see Norris is putting his certificate of the obvious to good use. It does tend to keep the captain sweet. And he has lasted for some time now. Longer than most.'

'And in a kite with a hundred and eighty h.p. engine,' added Tibbit, still in disbelief.

'At least you know what the captain wants,' added Maloney. 'And let's not forget this man came up against von Richthofen and lived to tell the tale about it. In that kite with that unreliable Wolseley engine.'

Norris nodded. 'And that is actually on two occasions.' 'Who is von Richthofen?' asked Tibbit.

'He's often called the Red Baron by the front-line troops,' said Maloney. 'I thought everyone knew the German ace.'

'Is that the Red Baron's real name then?' Tibbit sounded excited and shocked at the same time. 'I've heard of the Red Baron, but I thought he was just a myth. I never knew his real name and that he was a real baron to boot. Is he one of those old-fashioned Prussian aristocrats? Like the ones we hear about in history?'

Maloney continued with a nervous air. 'Baron von Richthofen is no myth, Tibby. He and his flying circus are our pilots' worst nightmare. Our Red Baron nemesis is very real indeed. At the moment, he operates in the skies that our men fly through, and as such, the Baron has claimed many of our pilots lately.'

'So, when our lads go out there, they might meet the Red Baron?' Tibbit asked in awe and disbelief.

'To be sure, Tibby. The Red Baron and his flying circus are in this vicinity. And they are many ace pilots,' Maloney said.

'His kill tally is rising all the time,' added Cooper, then swigged his tea.

Norris sniffed and then added his opinion. 'As aristocrats go, he's of that old Prussian stock. But our Red Baron is young and enthusiastic. And as pilots go, this aristo is the full shilling, mate – he has flying skills that are second to none. I've heard pilots talk about him. I heard them say he was an enig—' He looked at Cooper for help.

'An enigma,' Cooper completed. 'The man is like a phantom wrapped in crimson canvas. He appears, strikes and moves off. He twists and turns on a sixpence, according to some pilots.'

'You sound as though you admire the man,' added Tibbit, a little shocked.

Cooper took a deep breath and nodded in agreement. 'I think it's fair to say we do, Tibby. But begrudgingly. Our Captain Polden and his observer dropped low as they reached the Australian lines not far from here. He flew over the trenches where the Ozzie troops are stationed. Those mad Ozzie soldiers salivate at this Prussian aristocrat. They love our airmen to bring a stray Hun over their positions and they'll fling all sorts of muck up at the unsuspecting Hun, but the Baron never takes the bait. He knows when to turn away to live and fight another day. That's how Captain Polden escaped the infamous von Richthofen twice. Both times by dropping low when he reached the Ozzie trenches.'

'You would have to make sure the ole Ozzie clocks you right,' added Maloney. 'Because you don't want to be shot down by friendly fire.'

'Well, that doesn't seem very friendly to me,' gasped Tibbit, listening to the descriptions of the Red Baron with great amazement and terror. 'A crimson phantom! Is that how we refer to this man in his killing machine?'

'Every plane is a killing machine, Tibby,' Norris said.

'I'm just thinking. Imagine going through such an ordeal with the Red Baron and his mates, managing to come out alive, and then when you drop low over the Ozzie lines, you end up getting shot at by our own blokes.' Tibbit was bemused. He hadn't thought too much about accidental friendly fire.

'Your Ozzie wouldn't mean it. Friendly fire can sometimes happen accidently,' said Cooper.

Tibbit's eyes widened as he replied with comical sarcasm, 'Oh well, that makes me feel so much better. Sod all of this for a blooming lark.'

Maloney, Norris and Cooper chuckled at Tibbit's shock, and each man took a bite of carrot cake. Tibbit followed suit as they grinned at one another, munching their succulent bake. Each man gulped, and they took another swig of hot tea to wash the brief repast down. Then the conversation resumed.

Norris sniffed snootily. 'I would have thought our Captain Polden would turn for the duel in the air. He seems to know his machine. He's a good pilot – one of our best.'

'The Red Baron knows his machine too. I think Captain Polden was wise to lure this legendary ace close to the Ozzie lines. But the Baron knows the score. The German ace is very cunning, according to the captain,' said Cooper.

'Of course he is. We know the way of things, working here on the planes,' added Norris. 'How many of our men have we seen go out and not come back this month? It's only the 5th of April and we've already lost two aircrews from this squadron. The other airfields tell the same story. I can't understand how they keep getting new recruits to fly these kites. They turn up burning with enthusiasm, and then you can see that eagerness die within them. They come back with what they've seen in aerial combat and the wind is taken well and truly out of their sails.'

Maloney sighed and replied, 'Well now, I can't say as I blame the poor sods. Makes me wonder what sort of speeches they've been fed before they come out here. Look at some of the pilots we've had over the last year. Gradually losing faith and getting more into the ways of drinking when they're back at their officers' mess. Then one day, off they go. Never to return.'

'Did the drinking part include the bloke who taught you about the camera?' asked Tibbit.

'Of course it did, Tibby. That bloke put on a brave face. Young Cadet Observer Brett. He was eighteen. Here for about three weeks. Most of which he spent showing me how to work the camera.'

'He used to come in here often,' added Norris. 'A bit like Adams in that way.'

Cooper sighed. 'I can still remember that last morning when he came in here with Lieutenant Ashcroft. All happy and chatty. He'd been in the mess the previous evening and was pleased he had no hangover. He thought it was a good sign. Exactly twenty days he'd been here. He had a number of missions under his belt in that time and had shot down a Hun via his rear Lewis gun a few days prior. A confirmed kill too. Our Cadet Observer Brett thought he was among the seasoned chaps, as they were known. I suppose they try to convince themselves. He was a lad who tried to do good and achieve things. Lieutenant Ashcroft was full of praise for Brett's confirmed kill as well. Everything seemed to be going well for them. They were happy for a short-lived time. Then came that last morning they were in here, before their kite, like a couple of cats who'd got the cream.'

'What engine did they have?' asked Tibbit.

The other three mechanics were silent and looked at the new recruit. Then Maloney raised a humorous eyebrow and asked, 'Does it matter, Tibby?'

'Well no. I was just wondering about the good engines and the not so good engines in these Biffs. Is it Biffs or kites?'

Cooper sniffed. 'Biffs is what the aircrew call their Bristol F2B aircraft. We refer to all aircraft as kites. Only these Bristol aircraft are Biffs. It's an affectionate name.'

Maloney chuckled. 'And just for the book, Lieutenant Ashcroft and Cadet Observer Brett went down in a Wolseley Viper engine. One moment here and full of life, and the next moment, gone. God rest their souls.'

'And off they went,' Norris said, putting a cigarette to his lips and offering the pack about. 'I can still see their Biff bouncing along the grass and lifting off into the grey sky. It was a very chilly morning, and it was only just getting light.'

'That was back in the February,' added Maloney. 'Out they went, never to return.'

Tibbit asked hopefully, 'Surely the Hun is losing pilots too?'

'That's not really the point, Tibby,' Norris replied. 'It doesn't give much comfort to a pilot if he knows that a brace of Huns are going down in flames when he's on his way down too. There are probably Hun air mechanics on their side of the line having the same chat as we are.'

Tibbit sighed and took a deep breath, then asked, 'How does the Red Baron get so many kills? Why has no one matched him?' He had declined a cigarette and bit another chunk of his carrot cake.

Maloney raised his eyebrows. 'I've been told the Red Baron flies above dogfights and looks for stragglers. He likes to dive down upon them with the sun on his back and dazzle the observer.'

'Swoops down with twin Spandau guns blazing away,' Cooper added. 'The number of our lads he's claimed in dogfights is frightening. But I still think someone will get the better of him one day. No one can have that much luck.'

Maloney shrugged. 'I think the Baron von Richthofen has something extra special. Something more than just luck. I think he's remarkably skilled. He must be to have claimed so many kills. But I think he might run out of such good fortune one day.'

'How many has this Red Baron brought down?' asked Tibbit.

'It's hard to say the exact number between unconfirmed kills and confirmed kills,' answered Cooper.

'I reckon over a hundred if we included all unconfirmed and confirmed kills together,' added Norris.

Maloney laughed. 'The Baron von Richthofen is good, but not that good, Norris. He's a living legend and people give extra merit to such embodiment—'

'Embodiment! Blooming heck, Maloney, have you stuck a chopped-up dictionary in this birthday cake?' Norris cut in, chuckling and looking at his half-eaten lump of cake.

'As I was saying before being rudely interrupted, the Baron von Richthofen has become an embodiment of legend. This is for sure and with this comes all sorts of exaggerated claims. I would be doubting the ace has shot down such a tally of aircrew. His luck would run out before he could reach half that number.'

'I'm afraid I'm with Norris on this one, Dermot. I believe he has easily got in excess of half that number concerning just confirmed kills,' replied Cooper with a serious tone. 'Captain Polden believes the ace has reached such a number of kills, and I think our captain's estimate is credible.'

Maloney was genuinely surprised. He had a begrudging respect for the officer's integrity. The man never cast false aspersions. 'Does Captain Polden really believe the kill numbers hype then? Does he think the Red Baron has shot down one hundred of our aircraft?'

Cooper took a swig of his tea, then said, 'I don't think the captain said he believed that Baron von Richthofen had a hundred confirmed kills. But he may be nearing that mark with unconfirmed kills added to the overall tally. Those are almost his words. Obviously, I can't remember the exact way he said this but those estimates were his own.'

'So, a hundred confirmed and unconfirmed kills is speculation from Captain Polden?' asked Maloney.

Cooper sighed hesitantly and replied, 'The captain's exact words were, "close to one hundred planes brought down" between the confirmed and unconfirmed. I know it's only speculation—'

'Speculation!' called Norris. 'Not you as well? I ask again, have you mixed a dictionary into the cake's ingredients, Maloney?'

'Stick a sock in it, Norris,' said Cooper, then looked back at Maloney. 'It is just speculation, but Captain Polden thinks this Richthofen is a bit special on the air ace front. He says there's been nothing like him up to now. We have some very good pilots and so do the Froggies, but our Red Baron is something else.'

'We never stop hearing about his flying circus lot,' added Norris. 'Jagdgeschwader I is its proper name, I think. The whole squadron has talent. There are other names besides the Baron. All those Fokker DR1 triplanes. A travelling circus moving along the lines here and there, pitching tents in fields anywhere they can. They seem to be like a moving caravan of big names following Baron von Richthofen's red triplane. They travel where needed and then move on somewhere else along the lines when the occasion demands.'

'I've heard that only the Baron's plane is completely red, while the others adopt some bits in red with individual patterns and designs around their own planes,' said Norris, wanting to redeem his standing in the conversation.

'Norris is right,' Cooper assured him. 'According to Captain Polden, the other Jagdgeschwader I aircraft have varied patterns. They might have some small parts in red, like a frontal engine casing, red wheel carriages and struts. But the fuselage may be elaborately decorated. I think that's why they're referred to as the flying circus.'

'Well, I'm sure other planes in the outfit do just that,' added Maloney. 'And right now, the circus has come to this area of the front. Lieutenant Adams says as much. All manner of Fokker DR1 triplanes coming up to greet them every time our blokes go on recces.'

'So, they're not all red?' asked Tibbit.

Maloney shrugged and replied, 'Lieutenant Adams reckons they're different colours with red aspects thrown in here and there. Only the Baron's is completely red though. I think he said the tail fin is white with the black cross. He said the other Huns do include some red parts on their planes as mentioned already. This is done on all the planes in Jagdgeschwader I because the other pilots don't want their Red Baron singled out as a prize target. How true this really is, I can't say for sure. It may be a squadron thing, but it also makes sense.'

'Bits of red here and there on otherwise colourful planes might not make us think they are Baron von Richthofen,' added Cooper.

The telephone rang inside the small inner tent office. All four mechanics looked at one another. The major was with Lieutenant Adams. What did anyone in the main office want with the air mechanics?

'Who's going to get that?' asked Norris. He had an aversion to the telephone, a contraption way above his station.

'I'll get it,' said Maloney with a quiet note of irritation.

As the young Irishman headed to a smaller, draped tent office, Cooper said, 'I've got a bad feeling about this.'

Norris looked at his workmate. 'Surely they wouldn't do this to the bloke on his twentieth birthday?'

Tibbit looked on as Maloney stepped into the office. The ringing stopped as he answered the telephone.

MAJOR LAWS' OFFICE

There was a knock before the aide-de-camp put his head through the open door. Major Laws stopped writing and looked up at his secretary.

'Yes, Carruthers.' The major seemed vexed.

'Lieutenant Adams reporting, sir.'

'Very good, Carruthers. Show him in and please arrange for some tea to be fetched.'

'Yes, sir.' Carruthers disappeared and in came the pilot, Lieutenant Adams.

'Please be seated, Lieutenant Adams. I'm just sending Carruthers to get the necessary on the tea front.'

'Oh, thank you, sir.' Adams was now very worried. Tea and biscuits were not a good sign. Major

Laws showing a kindly disposition was never a positive thing in his experience. It usually meant something was wanted. Something one would not normally give. Something a little more than most were prepared to offer, but that no one could refuse to give. Everyone was in the forces. Why pretend to ask when there was only one answer allowed? Adams ran his tongue along his bottom lip and decided that their good English manners were sometimes patronising. A bit like being stabbed by a pleasant-looking person with a constant smiling face.

'Got a spot of bad news, old chap,' Major Laws began. 'Oh,' was all Adams could say in reply.

'I'm afraid that Sullivan fellow – the new observer-in-training chap – has just been carted off in an ambulance. A grumbling appendix seems to be the problem. The poor fellow collapsed outside less than half an hour ago. The long and the short of it all, Adams – we're down on observers, dash it all, old boy. Completely down and the new batch is not due for a couple of days. The observers we do have are already allocated. Putting our cards on the table, we need an observer from somewhere at short notice. We are pushed to the limit at this precise moment, and I need the full complement for this next mission.'

'I see, sir. May I take it that the observers we do have are already assigned and unable to take on what

Sullivan and I had to do? Are their assignments as important as the mission that I might assume we're going on?'

Major Laws cleared his throat and continued, 'I'm afraid we cannot offload your task onto another aircrew, Lieutenant Adams. I can see only one course of action at such short notice. What I must insist upon is highly irregular and at extraordinary short notice. One of the air mechanics 1st class. There are three in your hangar. AM ones – Maloney, Cooper and Norris. Of the three, Maloney seems the soundest. I have his file here. The man is very enthusiastic about learning new things. He trained on the Lewis gun, just like everyone else, but this chap Maloney is good with the Morse code transmitter. He knows the clock code too. Then there is the photographic training he did with the late Lieutenant Greenway.'

Lieutenant Adams carefully cut in. 'I think that was the late Cadet Observer Brett for photography, sir. I think Lieutenant Greenway was the Morse code transmitter.'

Major Laws frowned and picked up his spectacles and looked back at his file. 'So it was, Adams. I have both the late officers' appraisals of the mechanic and I've mixed them up. Greenway for Morse code and Brett for photography. Well, both highly recommended Maloney. I'm looking at this chap's file and I think the man is an absolute glutton for knowledge. In fact, I think Maloney would make a first-class observer if given the chance. I'm of the opinion we should give this air mechanic an opportunity to make it as an observer. What are your thoughts?'

There was a knock on the door and Carruthers opened it for a young orderly who came in nervously holding a tray with a teapot, a milk jug, cups and saucers plus a plate of biscuits.

'Ah, the refreshment,' replied Laws with delight. 'In you come, young man.'

Adams' mind raced. He knew Maloney had no interest in going up as an observer. He didn't blame the young mechanic. Maloney had cursed learning the Morse code transmitter and clock check sometime back, now that the reality of flying had hit home for all the mechanics. Adams would have liked to help Maloney by playing down his abilities, but Major Laws had known Maloney before he had arrived at the airfield. The senior officer peddled the notion of sending the mechanic up as though he was giving away an opportunity. Did the major expect Maloney to be grateful? Was he really doing the air mechanic a favour?

Major Laws moved his file aside and allowed the orderly to place the tea tray and contents upon the desk.

'Splendid, splendid. Thank you, young man.' Major Laws looked up at Adams as the would-be tea boy made off. Carruthers nodded and closed the door. Laws leaned back in his chair and proffered his hand. 'You may pour, Adams. Mine is tea with milk and no sugar.'

'Very good, sir. The same as myself.' Lieutenant Adams stood and carefully poured the major his tea.

'I don't want others about while we discuss this, even the tea boy. This is an important corner-cutting exercise. You may have wanted Captain Polden in here. He would usually be saddled with this responsibility when I'm at another airfield. However, seeing as this new acting cadet observer would be your responsibility, I thought it proper to run it by you first. I'm certain Captain Polden would not like this idea – I will overrule him on this matter. I also know it's not fitting to be saying this to a subordinate officer concerning his captain, but blast it, time is of the essence, and I would sooner have the discussion with Captain Polden after I sort this with you.'

'Of course, sir,' Adams replied and then lied. 'I have to say, I was not too keen on Maloney's use of the Morse code transmitter.' It was a gentle stab in the dark. Maybe he could dissuade the major from making his decision and he wasn't comfortable with his squadron leader being left out of the debate.

Major Laws looked puzzled as his grey moustache drooped around his displeased lips. 'I didn't know that you had observed or knew about Maloney's use of the Morse code transmitter. Where did you gain such knowledge?'

'Oh...' Adams stuttered. 'Just overheard chatter between the air mechanics, sir. Norris and Cooper said as much when I first came here, sir.'

'Blast it all, Adams, I wouldn't take much notice of those two urchins. A pair of earth lovers. That's all they'll ever be. Dashed good mechanics, but no men of the blue, so to speak. They're probably just envious.' The major pulled up his open file and continued. 'Norris failed the Morse code transmitter and Cooper just scraped by. Young Maloney knocked the pair of them into cocked hats.'

'Really, sir.' Adams feigned interest as Laws turned the file around and showed him the glowing testaments written by the late Lieutenant Greenway and below the photography credits, the deceased Cadet Observer Brett. Greenway and Brett were the flying team that had gone down in their burning plane a couple of months back. He also knew that Norris and Cooper would deliberately lack enthusiasm on the Morse code transmitter, map-reading and clock code-reporting. All this before learning aerial photography. These seasoned air mechanics had seen too many airmen come and go during the air war. They were more than happy to play the ignorant fools where flying was concerned. There was no reason to mention that he had overheard Cooper and Norris telling Maloney why they had deliberately failed the test for such undertakings. He had also heard Maloney saying he wished that he had never been so enthusiastic about learning the skills that a trained observer would know.

'I'm not going to hold the lad back,' Laws continued. 'I think the enthusiastic young man deserves this opportunity and I'm dashed well going to give the lad a go.'

'I'm sure AM Maloney will be very pleased, sir.' There was a tone of sarcasm in Adams' reply, but it was for him, and he knew Major Laws would be oblivious. The old officer had a rather thick skin when it suited him.

Adams looked on and smiled, listening with a polite countenance as the major waffled on about giving the young NCO ranks a chance. Did the major believe he was doing Maloney a favour, or was he just pretending to? An act of offering a good prospect to a man that Laws would normally decide was beneath such a station in life. What fickle ways came about in wartime. All the normal rules were there to be broken. Lieutenant Adams decided that Major Laws was not a man to offer favours. He was a complete class snob, and he was using Maloney as a scape goat for his little dilemma, something dreadful and carefully packaged as an opportunity.

'Let me show you what I would like you and this Maloney chap to do.' Laws got up, holding his cup of tea. Adams complied and did likewise as he was shown to another large table at the back of the major's office. The whole surface of this large table was covered with aerial photographs. Some of the photos were overlapping, and all seemed to be taken at the same height. Each photo of a trench line was laid over another, with the trench lines connecting at the right place. It was like a giant jigsaw puzzle connected together, forming a photomap of the front and the various installations behind German lines.

'I want correct guidance via the clock check for this gun position here.' Laws pointed at a photograph of a gun emplacement behind the lines. 'Using the clock code system which our lad Maloney is competent on and the Morse code transmitter he's also competent on, I want readings for our artillery units to fire at. Keep giving the correctional readings until our artillery chaps hit the target. Other planes will be directing at other targets, and you will also have a squadron of Sopwith Camels and a few SPADs. Obviously, the Hun will send up the usual reception. We need correct targeting and once the hits are made, we would like new photographs. We also need you and this Maloney back in one piece.'

Lieutenant Adams took a swig of tea. Laws did the same and continued. 'I wouldn't be too concerned about Maloney's reaction. I'm sure he'll be delighted seeing as it's his birthday today. I bet he'll be busting a gut to be up there. What a grand twentieth for the lad. I'm sure it'll give him something to tell his grandchildren one day.' The major chuckled.

'I'm sure Maloney will be overwhelmed, sir.' Adams was certain that Maloney wouldn't be too ecstatic concerning his promotion to Acting Observer.

'I'll tell you what I'm going to do, Adams. Seeing as it is the lad's twentieth, I'll call the hangar and have him come here. Show him this photo compilation and give him this great news. We can make an exception for a lower rank concerning this. A little birthday treat with a cup of tea and biscuit to boot!'

Adams felt quite cold as he smiled. How could Major Laws possibly think Maloney, a competent mechanic with over a year's experience, would want to go up against such diabolical odds? 'I'm sure Maloney will be delighted, sir,' he lied.

'I'm sure Maloney will do well, and you'll soon have a dependable observer. A homegrown one, Adams. There's a lot to be said for that.'

'Of course, sir.' Adams reasoned that Maloney would survive this mission. But he and Maloney knew there would be a limited period of time before being shot down. Adams knew his time might come soon. He would try to talk anyone out of flying during this war. The romantic adventure of the dogfight was an illusion that quickly disappeared once the actual experience was witnessed first-hand. He had said as much to all three of the air mechanics in the hangar. Most of all, to Maloney. He stared down at the aerial photograph of the gun emplacement as Major Laws picked up his desk telephone.

'Put me through to Hangar Three,' said Laws. He waited for some time before the phone was answered.

Adams surveyed the entire ad hoc map of various photos aligned and overlapping in the right places – roads and trenches continuing across and onto the next photo frame. He had seen it all before but still thought it was stunning. His attention was diverted when the major spoke.

'Ah, is that you, Maloney? A happy birthday, lad,' he said.

There came the sound of crackling, incoherent speech at the other end. Laws looked back to Adams and nodded approvingly before continuing.

'All good to know, Maloney. Now, I would like you to get over here to my compound as quickly as possible. There is something that Lieutenant Adams and I would like to run past you.' He put the telephone down and rubbed his hands briskly. Things were going swimmingly well for the major as he pressed his buzzer.

Once again, Carruthers poked his head round the door as Major Laws said, 'Get another cup and saucer for Maloney. After all, it is the lad's birthday.'

Adams wanted to say, *My word! You're pushing the boat out, Major.* But he bit his tongue and stayed silent. He could tell that Carruthers might be thinking of something along the same lines.

THE DREADFUL BIRTHDAY PRESENT

Maloney walked out of the narrow tented room within the vast canvas hangar. His face had gone white. All noticed the stunned expression in his eyes.

Cooper and Norris fell silent and slowly stood up. Both men frowned with concern for their friend. Tibbit slowly stood too. He looked from Maloney to Cooper and then to Norris.

Norris spoke first. 'Oh, for God's sake, Dermot! Please don't tell us the major did it?'

'Not over the telephone. But I think our major is about to, that's for sure. I'm still pinching myself. I'm certain they'll want me to go up with Lieutenant Adams. Major Laws has not exactly said that but why would they want an aircraft mechanic to go over to the compound and listen to two officers yarn about officer things? I suppose I'm in for the dreaded cup of tea and a digestive biscuit. I would sooner it be some of those biscuits with flies in.'

'Flies?' Tibbit frowned in disgust.

'Garibaldi biscuits, Tibby,' Norris replied.

Cooper cussed, 'Oh Christ, Dermot. Why didn't you fail that blooming Morse code transmitter course. You'd have been useless to them without that under your belt.'

'Those words are not really helpful now, Mr Cooper.' Maloney always became formal when vexed. 'To be sure, they're of no use at all. I've been a blooming silly boy, and telling me this with hindsight is pointless.' He then looked directly at Tibbit. 'Take note, Tibby. This is what happens when you are enthusiastic and learn too much. You'll end up in one of those blooming Biffs. Trust us and learn from this. The blooming romance should be well and truly knocked off you concerning flying in aircraft. You'll see the aircrew come and go...'

'Many going and never coming back again,' added Cooper.

'Would you lads be doing me a favour now?' asked Maloney.

'Of course, Dermot,' replied Norris.

'Just say what you want, and we'll do it, Dermot,' added Cooper.

Maloney sighed. 'Give that Biff I've been working on another once over please? Make sure those Lewis drum magazines are filled with the full ninety-seven rounds?'

'Of course, we will,' said Cooper. 'We'll also pray that they're calling you over for another reason.'

'Well now, what might that be, Cooper? A nice birthday present. I wouldn't put it past Major Laws to pretend this is a big birthday gift. I'll have to pretend I'm overcome by the joy of it all. I don't think the major lives out here in the world we see, even though he must realise how many airmen don't return. That man must have grown hard to it all. He sends aircrew out all the time knowing many won't return.'

Norris added, 'We'll look over the lieutenant's Biff and we'll also make sure the ninety-seven-round drums are in the racks of your cockpit. Do you want that thinner "good luck" forty-seven-round drum too?'

Cooper nodded his agreement. 'That might come in useful. It's only a trick drum, but it's a cheeky cheat yet to be used on the Hun. Just right for a fledgling observer to try when at the back with a big "grab a load of this" Lewis gun. You know how close the Hun likes to get before releasing a short well-aimed burst.'

Maloney nodded and replied with a smile. 'Especially if he thinks he has time to get in close during a change of magazine. Why not have some little trick or surprise on standby? I'm hoping it won't be necessary but why not be prepared?'

All three watched Maloney walk out of the hangar and along the turf towards the complex of wooden huts, where Major Laws would be waiting with Lieutenant Adams.

Tibbit, Cooper and Norris watched for a while the retreating form of Maloney. It was Tibbit who sighed first and began the new conversation.

'So, I presume this kite is the one that Lieutenant Adams and our Dermot Maloney will go up in?'

'That's right, young Tibby. We'll also look at the bigger Lewis drums for the ninety-seven bullets. We keep the best ones nicely primed with inner spring workings in tip top condition, mate.' Norris was walking about the Bristol F2B while Cooper got the ladder and placed it on the fuselage just below the observer's hatch.

As Cooper climbed the steps and investigated the observer's cockpit, he called down to the new recruit. 'Tibby. Do us a favour, mate? Go over to that stores counter and fetch the thicker Lewis drum magazines. Put them on the work bench here. About ten drums and then four big boxes of the .303 bullets. They're all under the counter over there – we had them fresh from the stores this morning. When you've done that, bring three of those chairs over and we'll start to load these chunky drum magazines. We've done our plane's magazines. Captain Polden and Elliott will be flying that kite this afternoon.'

'But what if Maloney isn't going up?' asked Norris. 'After all, it might be for something different. We'll have to unload them all.'

'Wouldn't we be happy to unload them all?' said Cooper. 'Meaning that Maloney isn't going up?'

'Point taken,' Norris replied as he ran his hand gently along the ailerons of the lower starboard wing. 'Maloney has this old bird in good order. He's been over everything.'

For a few minutes the men went about their individual tasks. Tibbit dutifully placed the thick circular magazine drums of the Lewis gun upon a spare work bench. Ten in all stacked in threes with one in front of the first chair he put around the bench. He got two more chairs ready then returned to the counter and fetched four boxes of weighty bullets. Each chest was the size of a shoe box and within each box were smaller grease wrapped packages of .303 bullets.

Cooper came down from his ladder and took the first seat. He looked back to Norris and called, 'Can you see anything?'

'Nothing untoward,' Norris replied. 'You know what Maloney's like with the lieutenant's kite. This plane is the full shilling all the way.'

'Let's be loading these ninety-seven drums then,' said Cooper.

Tibbit frowned as he looked at the Lewis gun magazine's circular thickness. 'At the training school we had the smaller magazines for forty-seven bullets.'

'The army tends to use them,' said Norris as he arrived at the bench and sat down. He picked up one of the chunky drum magazines and pulled over a case of bullets. 'Up there in the blue, you need something that will last a little longer than usual.'

'We were told about the ninety-seven-round drum magazines,' added Tibbit. 'We just never used them back at the training ground. This is the first time I've seen them. They're big old girls, aren't they?'

'I presume they told you about the short, sharp bursts thing?' asked Cooper.

'They did,' Tibbit replied. 'We also practised it. No continuous rapid fire.'

'That's the one,' added Norris. 'The air-cooled induction on the Lewis is good. But never push your luck with continuous machine-gun fire. Aim, squeeze out three or four, then stop – aim, squeeze another three or four then stop. Besides, the Hun on your tail will be jostling up and down from side to side and a stop to aim makes his job more difficult.'

Cooper smiled and nodded his agreement. 'That little stop and aim again helps the air-cooled induction. Lessens the chance of overheating. You don't want a case failure when up there facing a Hun fighter, do you now, Tibby?'

'No,' sniggered Tibbit. 'It must be difficult to remember all of these little things in the heat of a dogfight.' He looked down and inserted another bullet.

'It's best that an observer remembers, Tibby. We need to give Dermot the best chance possible if he's going up. But the memory and order of things is down to him.' Norris sighed and looked outside the hangar. Airfield personnel were moving about their various chores and a muddy old truck drove past.

Cooper looked at his workmate and tried to console him. 'I know you're concerned about Dermot, Norris. You're hoping it's all of us overreacting, but our Tibby here saw Lieutenant Adams' observer Sullivan carted off in an ambulance. We know there are no spare observers, and our Dermot has all the necessary courses under his belt. Now he has a telephone call to report to Major Laws. You don't need the brains of Lloyd George to work that one out, do you?'

'No, I don't need any help from the prime minister,' Norris agreed. 'I just hope it's something else, but let's face it, there's nothing else such a call could be for.'

'Who did you say would fly the other kite that you lads were working on?' asked Tibbit, carefully loading the rounds into the big drum magazine. Watching each bullet slide into the circular magazine. He lifted the drum up and could see the inner workings as the stacked bullet's shell casing neatly moved along the inner circumference of the circular drum each time a new shell was inserted.

'The airman mentioned it was Captain Polden and his observer, Cadet Elliott,' Norris replied. 'Both good blokes. Captain Polden is a stern, dependable type. Elliott is a recruit like yourself. He's been out on a few flights now. He arrived a few days back.'

'So, I can presume Captain Polden is a good and skilful pilot?' asked Tibbit. 'You said he's escaped from the Red Baron on two occasions.'

'Our Captain Polden is a very good pilot indeed. But they still burn and fall, Tibby. The captain is a big fan of flying low over the Ozzie trenches when returning home. Any enemy pilot that wants to chase him will get the over-enthusiastic Ozzies giving it some serious large with the anti-aircraft guns and their own soldiers firing their rifles up at anything mad enough to fly low. Hundreds of pot-shots from all directions are likely to hit something. So, you never can tell. Problem is that our blokes run a high risk of getting shot down by our own side. Friendly fire and all.'

Tibbit looked concerned. 'Well that seems very risky to me.'

Norris and Cooper laughed at the young recruit as he lifted the drum magazine again and looked at the open underneath and the progress of the stacked shells.

'Well, it does involve a certain amount of buttock-clenching.' Cooper laughed.

Norris nodded humorously. 'But when you have a lively Hun on your tail, Tibby – you might want to take the chance of a nice little cheek-clench. The Ozzies are getting mindful of us chaps flying low over their positions. They think it's a great sport. You can hear them cheering when our blokes fly over, so I'm told.'

'The good old Ozzies.' Cooper chuckled.

'Blimey! That all sounds rather jolly,' said Tibbit with a touch of sarcasm.

Again, there was the usual laughter. It was clear the old hands were fond of their new recruit. He had a dry sense of humour and seemed relaxed with his fellow mechanics.

'We call it the Polden manoeuvre,' said Norris.

'The Polden manoeuvre?' Tibbit repeated it while inserting another round into the drum magazine. 'Have the Ozzies ever brought a plane down during this Polden manoeuvre?'

Cooper snorted. 'I don't think so. No Hun is daft enough to fly so low in pursuit of a kill. They'll run the risk of becoming a cheap kill for our ground forces.'

Norris nodded in agreement, loading his drum magazine. 'Also, as far as I know, the Polden manoeuvre has only been performed on two occasions—'

'And that was by Captain Polden.' Tibbit smiled as he cut in.

'There you go, Tibby,' Cooper said as he looked at Norris. 'No pulling the wool over Tibby's eyes.'

'Don't get too clever, Tibby. You'll get noticed by a toff-off,' said Cooper, giggling.

'What's a toff-off?'

'I think it means a toff officer,' added Norris. 'And it's not a regular saying. Our Cooper often tries to invent his own slang.'

Cooper looked put out. 'What's wrong with toff-off for a hoity-toity officer then?'

'It's a bit pants,' Tibbit said. He felt very relaxed and at ease in the company of his two fellow mechanics. 'Did Captain Polden invent the saying "Polden manoeuvre"? That sounds a bit pants too. I'm sure other flyers along the lines may have done such things. Perhaps the Huns do too. Drop low over their own lines.'

'Does pants mean not very good?' Norris chuckled. He looked at Cooper and added, 'Pants is a nice little invention. Better than toff-off for an officer, matey boy.'

Cooper looked indignant and sneered, 'So then, Tibby, our Captain Polden won't be too pleased when he finds out his Polden manoeuvre saying is put in the framework of pants. We'll say it was done on the Tibby-omiter of crass sayings.'

'He'll be ever so upset, will the captain,' added Norris, chuckling.

Tibbit inserted another .303 bullet into his drum magazine and raised an eyebrow. He was feeling very at home with the banter and enjoyed the camaraderie. Yet one of them was going to do something much more hazardous than bullet-loading.

Tibbit decided to change the subject. 'How many airmen have you seen come and go then?'

Cooper and Norris went silent for a moment as they thought about the question. Norris raised his eyebrows, uncertain where to begin.

Cooper tried to answer. 'A fair number, to be honest, Tibby. We've been lucky with Polden. He's been around for a little while. Elliott's very lucky to have been placed with him. Elliott is probably due for a nice little run with such a good pilot. A thinking man, is the captain. Spots things and acts very quickly, by all accounts. Not many of the aircraft we've worked on are still about. As I said, many have been lost with their aircrews. Some have survived and are still about – they're just in other hangars now. However, you have to get over those we've worked with and lost. It does no good to dwell. We've seen them climb into their kites, putting on their brave faces to fly off and never to return. You have to harden to that sort of thing. We've seen some smashing fellas come and go. I think you can tell the ones that won't last too long. Am I right, Norris?'

Norris breathed in through his flared nostrils as though he struggled with the memory. 'I'm afraid you're right, Coop. We've seen some sad things, Tibby. And mark my words, so will you, matey. I think a mechanic does get a strange sense of pilots as we see more and more of them come and go.'

'Do you think Lieutenant Adams is a man like Captain Polden?

Could he be like this pilot whose kite you work on?'

This time both men sighed reluctantly before Cooper chanced to reply. 'Sadly, I don't think so, Tibby.'

Norris nodded and added, 'I don't think our Dermot does either. Lieutenant Adams is a good bloke, but despite his devil-may-care appearance, the man has that little edge to him. His nerves are strained, as are all pilots that take flights day in and day out. I think the lieutenant's days are numbered and I think he knows it. Dermot knows it too and now he's likely to be going up with him as an observer. Our Dermot could end up sharing his pilot's lot.'

'So, Captain Polden is a survivor and Lieutenant Adams is not?' Tibbit frowned, trying to imagine the constant fear that all the aircrew must live with.

'I think so,' Cooper admitted.

'I do too,' added Norris. 'But we do get things wrong. We've seen some good pilots fall and burn and others unfancied are still here. I didn't expect Lieutenant Adams to last as long as he has. But then yesterday, Cadet Observer Sullivan told me that Lieutenant Adams becomes a different man up in the blue. Maybe he is? Perhaps the nerves seep out when his feet are back on the ground.'

'Let's hope so then,' said Tibbit. 'Perhaps he saves his best for the sky. He seemed a bit too pally-pally for an officer. I know I only met him thirty minutes ago, but I did notice his strange unofficer-like manner when joking to me. When it comes to oily rags like us, being overly jocular doesn't sit well. It wouldn't do back at the training school.'

'You'll find a few pilots are like that, once you get out there.' Cooper nodded, contemplating the matter. 'Maybe Lieutenant Adams is at his best up in the sky. That's one part of his game that we don't see.'

'It would be a plus for any new observer with the lieutenant if this is so,' Norris concluded.

'Let's hope so then.' Tibbit smiled and continued loading his drum magazine.

For a short time, things went silent as each man finished loading their first drum magazine with the full ninety-seven bullets. Cooper took three loaded magazines and put them on a trolley by the ladder leading to the observer's cockpit. He then came back and took a fresh empty drum and began loading again. Tibbit and Norris were already a few shells into their second drums.

'I'm wondering how long von Richthofen and his flying circus will be around this stretch of the lines before they move further along the front in search of fresh kills,' Cooper said.

'I can't see that lot going anytime soon. The blooming Huns seem to be enjoying themselves,' Norris spat indignantly.

Tibbit looked up. 'The Prussian aristocrat – our Red Baron. Is he as hard as nails with no pity? I just get this image of Huns being this way.'

'Your Hun is no different from us, Tibby,' Norris replied, scrutinising his bullet-loading.

'This Baron seems to have a flair for killing our blokes,' continued Tibbit.

Cooper answered, 'I don't think it's anything personal, Tibby. Von Richthofen has to be hard to survive. He's no different from our blokes on that score. Kill or be killed. This is not a grand adventure, Tibby. These blokes are out to fight deadly duels in the air. There are no prizes for the silver medallists. It's gold every time or bust.'

Norris nodded and continued with his own hearsay knowledge. 'A few of the Hun circus pilots have gone down in flames too, Tibby. Even your Hun is not invincible. One of their high-flying aces went down in flames last month near Lens. Hans-Joachim Buddecke was his name. He ran into some of our Sopwith Camels. Went down with his silver medal. Like most flyers, he ran out of luck.'

'Our lads had old Hans for breakfast,' added Cooper, matter of fact in his manner. 'He was a good pilot, by all accounts. Had a Blue Max to boot.'

'A Blue Max?' Tibbit was inquisitive.

'I think its proper name is called a Pour le Mérite,' said Norris.

'That sounds French to me,' replied Tibbit. 'Why would a Hun call their award by a Froggie-sounding name?'

'Perhaps it's a Latin-sounding name. I can't tell the difference between French and Latin unless it's being sung by Catholic priests. Dermot Maloney might know. He's from Ireland, and their Catholic priests might say things in Latin.'

'Well, whatever,' said Tibbit impatiently. 'So, I take it this Pour le Mérite is called a Blue Max? And is this a high and important award? Like a Victoria Cross?'

In unison, Cooper and Norris looked most offended. 'No!' they both replied cuttingly and full of British bias.

'What a blooming liberty,' scoffed Norris indignantly.

While Cooper continued, 'Nothing in the entire world and in any army is higher than a Vicky Cross, Tibby. Surely you know that?'

'Well,' Tibbit stuttered. 'It is one of Germany's highest awards. I'm sure they don't give Blue Max medals out like toffees.'

'It is a very high honour and I think your Hun must score a number of kills before getting such an award,' replied Norris, calming down from the affront of comparing a Victoria Cross to a foreign medal.

'Why is it sometimes called the Blue Max instead of Pour le Mérite?' asked Tibbit.

Cooper was quick to answer. 'Oh, I know this one. The medal has the informal name of Blue Max because of the Huns' first ace to receive the award a couple of years back. By that I mean that this Pour le Mérite, which has been around for a long time, was only first awarded to the aircrew a couple of years back. An ace named Max Immelmann. Hence, the Blue Max in honour of Max Immelmann.'

'How did you get to know things like that?' asked Tibbit.

Cooper shrugged and answered, 'We got the news second-hand from another airfield. A captured Hun survived his plane crash and was the guest at that airfield where the pilot who shot him down was based. They all have enemy pilots over for a celebration if one survives. I believe the Huns do it if our blokes survive a crash too. Once the party is over, the Hun is put aboard a truck and taken to a POW camp. Well, one such prisoner spoke about honours and medals and told the story of why a Pour le Mérite got its name of Blue Max.'

'Oh, I see.' Tibbit continued to load his drum magazine.

'Didn't do the Hun ace much good. He went down in flames shortly after getting that medal,' added Norris.

'So, the informal name is in honour of this ace?' Tibbit raised his eyebrows.

'Yes, but only for aircrew,' Norris replied.

Cooper nodded and added, 'According to Captain Polden, the Red Baron wears such a medal when flying. The captain saw it via his rear-view mirror while being pursued. He saw the striking blue within the gold decor, just below the top of the Hun's buttoned collar.'

'Do they wear the medals when flying?' asked Tibbit.

'I think they like to,' replied Cooper. 'That live one they brought back to our mess for a drink had some. He didn't have a Blue Max but he did have two medals down his left side about here.' He pointed to the bottom of his ribs on the left side.

'That's right,' agreed Norris. 'The Hun pilot survived the crash and was brought back here to the officers' mess for a drinks session before being driven off to a POW camp.'

'I've heard about this sort of thing. Is it a tradition among air squadrons?' asked Tibbit.

'It is, Tibby,' Cooper replied. 'This German pilot was actually very honourable and took part in the tradition wholeheartedly. I think Captain Polden shot him down on this side of the lines. This Hun pilot told Captain Polden about his two medals. One was an Iron Cross – that black cross emblem they have on their aircraft within a white outline. Well, they also have a small badge like it, an old Teutonic knight thing, and below this Iron Cross was a black wound badge. The Hun loves decorations. They live for them.'

'I think a few have died for them too,' added Norris sarcastically.

'Awe,' replied Cooper. 'Sack the poet.'

'So, the Red Baron actually wore his Blue Max below his buttoned collar and Captain Polden saw it?' Tibbit frowned.

Cooper answered, 'That's what the captain said. He could make out the blue of the medal hanging below von Richthofen's fluttering scarf. The blue stood out. Probably has a personal orderly or batman polishing the medal before each flight.'

'You make the Red Baron sound like a cavalier,' Tibbit said, sniggering. 'Some dandy of the sky.'

'Perhaps he is,' added Norris. 'I think aces of all countries begin to look this way. But the Huns build a reputation about their pilots and put them in newspapers. They're worshipped by all the Germans back home. As magnificent heroes.'

'We do too now,' said Tibbit.

'Yes, but we've only just started doing that. They never mentioned pilots by name unless they had been shot down and killed. Usually, obituaries and all. Now the government has cottoned on to the good publicity factor and like to mention our aces. Only because the Hun does.' Cooper smiled.

Norris continued to load his drum magazine, frowning and talking at the same time. 'That all goes out the window when one of the big aces goes down in flames. Could you imagine what it would be like if the Red Baron went down? How would the Hun report it?'

'I think von Richthofen will fall,' said Tibbit. 'The law of averages must be against him. Blue Max or not, the Hun will go down one day.'

Norris and Cooper stopped briefly. The young mechanic of less than half an hour was offering a rather high and mighty opinion about a complete greenie.

'Blimey, you've got some neck with your points of view, Tibby.' Cooper laughed at the cocksure attitude. 'Von Richthofen is no novice, mate. This Hun knows his onions like a kite. He can do some stunning things.'

'Don't be too harsh on our Tibby,' Norris cut in. 'After all, other aces on all sides have gone down in flames. Von Richthofen must be riding his luck. Maybe Tibby has a point. Just a matter of time.'

HAPPY BIRTHDAY, MALONEY

Once again, the orderly Carruthers put his head through the open door not wanting to enter the major's office completely.

'Air Mechanic 1st Class Maloney, sir.'

'Very good, Carruthers, send the chap in,' Laws replied.

The nervous-looking AM Dermot Maloney entered the office to find a smiling major and a concerned yet resigned-looking Lieutenant Adams. The young mechanic stood to attention in his new RAF forage cap that Carruthers had quickly exchanged for his old RFC cap. Maloney saluted as Major Laws returned with the usual unique high-ranking officer salute. A salute that the lower ranks would have been chastised for had they done such a thing.

'At ease, please, young Maloney. And a dashed happy birthday to you.'

'Thank you, sir.' Maloney could feel his skin crawling in anticipation of what was to come. He could see by Lieutenant Adams' emotionless features, a man reluctantly resigned to what was about to be said, that he already knew, and Maloney realised that Adams knew of his prior conclusion too.

'Take a seat, young man, and have a cup of tea. After all, it is your twentieth birthday and what better way to present such an opportunity.' Major Laws looked to Lieutenant Adams and then the teapot. The lieutenant instantly poured tea for his subordinate air mechanic.

Maloney could hear the little gremlin inside his mind, *Oh dear, oh dear. This is it! Not a good sign. When does an officer pour tea for a lacky?* He shut the distressing thought down.

'Take sugar, Maloney?' Adams asked kindly.

'No sugar – thank you, sir.' Maloney was seated and looking up nervously at Major Laws.

'Well, Maloney. Lieutenant Adams and I have been rather impressed by your ability to learn about the Morse code transmitter and the clock code. As you may already know, his observer, Sullivan, is off to hospital with suspected appendicitis. We are completely flummoxed for an observer with no new trainees available. You are the closest we have to a cadet observer. In fact, one might argue that you could be better qualified while working with added abilities under your belt. You have also done photographic work with other pilots.' Major Laws refrained from mentioning the name of the deceased Brett.

'I see, sir,' Maloney responded politely, accepting the teacup and saucer from Adams.

'The fact is that I need an observer at short notice and one that can be ready to go up very soon. About an hour's time, in fact. We have all the other kites ready for their missions, and we need you to go up with Lieutenant Adams for this little jaunt. You're being thrown in at the deep end, Maloney, but Lieutenant Adams and I have every confidence you will swim. You'll need to use the clock code and Morse transmitter to direct an artillery unit's fire at an enemy battery. Then some new photo shoots, followed by a quick dash home. There will be five Bristol F2Bs in all, each providing information about enemy gun emplacements for their own artillery contacts. Each observer is in contact with his own artillery unit, as you will be. You know of the Gosport system too, I presume? If not, it's straightforward enough to get to grips with and you'll be close to Lieutenant Adams throughout this mission.'

'Yes, sir. I do know the Gosport system,' Maloney replied.

'Good show! I know Lieutenant Adams is a big fan of this type of communication. Hates all that shoulder-tapping thing, isn't that right, Lieutenant Adams?'

'It is, sir,' Adams replied.

'You'll have a dozen Sopwith Camels accompanying you from another airfield. Lieutenant Adams knows the rendezvous routine. All you need to do is direct your artillery unit's fire at the enemy position via the Morse transmitter using the clock code. Our gun unit is good, and I'm sure they'll direct them to the target quickly.'

Maloney awkwardly took a gulp of his tea, feeling very self-conscious in front of the officers. And decided to ask a question of his own.

'How will I know the enemy target, sir?'

'A very good question,' Major Laws replied.

Maloney couldn't be sure if Major Laws was patronising him, and for a second or two there was an awkward silence. Maloney took a final gulp of the lukewarm tea and allowed Adams to take the cup and saucer from him.

'If you would like to come to this grand old table back here and look at all these photos. One of the benefits of high-altitude photographs – piece them altogether like a jigsaw puzzle, and this is what you get. A giant photographic map.'

Maloney followed Major Laws to the table, and his eyes widened. He was most impressed by the layout of photographs. It was indeed a giant photo puzzle resembling a bird's eye view. A real photo map.

'This is what you'll see from up there,' continued Major Laws. 'You will have this exact view. Can you see those three large sheds?' He pointed at three such buildings in one of the photos.

'Yes, sir.' Maloney was still taking in the impressive aerial view of the front lines and the area behind in the German-held territory.

'We like to leave some of these buildings up because they make for good land markers. Just to the left of these buildings at around eight o'clock if using the clock code system and imagining the buildings are our target, you'll see this crater here. It's covered in camouflage netting that looks like the earth.' He looked back at Adams and added, 'A dashed good job, actually.'

Adams stood next to Maloney. 'It is, sir. The Germans have done rather well. Looks like an empty bomb crater, but it's not.'

'Is the enemy's big gun beneath the netting, sir?' asked Maloney, understanding exactly what was required.

'It is, Maloney. That is what we need you to pinpoint to our chaps in the artillery unit.' Laws looked directly at Maloney.

'I'm certain I can do that, sir.' The young air mechanic was resigned. There was no way out of his predicament. And he knew what to do from the observer cockpit if he was in the air looking down at such a scene like the linked aerial photographic map before him.

'Very good, Maloney. You are now an acting observer for this mission and will go up with the lieutenant. Are you ready for this, young man?'

'Yes, sir. I am,' Maloney lied.

'Very good. That's all that needs to be said then. You and Lieutenant Adams will go to the stores and acquire a leather flying coat and the necessary sheepskin thigh boots. Also a flying cap and goggles plus any other things you need.' The major quickly scribbled out a requisition order, then looked up at Adams. 'I would like you to go to the stores with Maloney. The sergeant does tend to be under-enthusiastic about giving clothing out. An officer with this order from me cuts through all of that.' He turned to Maloney. 'Once you have these items, go back and prepare for this important assignment. It would have been abandoned but for the realisation of your recent training. Actually, I'm surprised you never mentioned this to me, Lieutenant Adams?'

For a moment, Adams was at a loss. What could he say? He cleared his throat and said, 'I had no idea that Air Mechanic 1st Class Maloney knew of all these relevant things, sir.'

'Understandable. I only remembered because I had heard the lad spoken of in glowing terms some time back.' Once again, Major Laws didn't mention the name of the dead aircrew who had told him.

The usual salutes followed as Adams and Maloney were dismissed. Each man was eager to leave the major's office. There was a polite acknowledgement from Carruthers sitting behind his desk as they left, and they walked out into the fresh air. Slowly, they made their way across the grass towards the stores – a small wooden compound a few yards away.

'Look, Maloney. I'm bloody sorry about all this. I did try to say you might not be up to the task, but the major was having none of it. I believe the late young Brett and Ashcroft spoke highly of you.'

Maloney sniggered. 'Did you say that to the major, sir? That I might not be up to the task? To be sure, I believe you would do a decent thing like that. I thank you for it. But here we are, sir. I'm of the mind to be thinking I can do what is required. But it's the flying part that I'll not be looking forward to. I'm not sure the head for heights is upon my shoulders.'

'I know you never wanted to go up in my Biff or anyone else's, come to that matter. You like the mechanics part of the job and have a well-developed loathing of flying in the things you maintain to a high standard. I can't blame you if flying is not your thing. I know you have seen pilots like me come and go. Doesn't inspire confidence, but here we are nonetheless. I also know you can do this mission where clock code and the Morse transmitter is concerned. But you'll also need to be good on the Lewis. The dash back, as Major Laws says, is not a cut and dry thing. That's where the price must often be paid. It's certain that our Hun will send up a bunch of party poopers. And it will be their good old flying circus, in my opinion. I would bet my last shilling on it.'

They were at the door of the old hut, and Adams opened it for Maloney to enter. There was no one at the counter, but this didn't bother the two men.

Maloney continued the discussion concerning the Lewis gun. 'I know I must do the aim, short burst – aim, short burst thing. You'll be doing all the manoeuvring and taking on anything to the front. I watch our tail and flanks, sir.'

A corporal in a khaki service dress jacket came casually through the door and stood with his hands on the counter, smiling at Maloney. 'What can I do for you, Dermot?'

'Just what's on this requisition chit, Corporal Ansell.' Lieutenant Adams turned and faced the man, whose face changed when he realised an officer was before him.

'I beg your pardon, sir.' Ansell instantly recognised the rank and stood to attention and saluted.

Adams returned the formality and put the requisition order on the table. 'No problem, Corporal. Our air mechanic 1st class is now an acting cadet observer and needs the necessary. Especially the sheepskin thigh boots.'

'Yes, sir,' replied Ansell. He turned back to Maloney and tentatively smiled. He didn't congratulate the mechanic on such a promotion. He knew Maloney well enough to assume it wouldn't be something he wanted. Instead, he said, 'I've got a very good pair of the thigh boots...' He didn't know how to address him properly with his new rank.

'Just call me Dermot or Maloney, Ansell. Let's not stand on ceremony just yet.' He chuckled.

'Of course, Dermot,' stuttered Ansell as he took the requisition order and went back into the doorway.

Moments later, Maloney was carrying his new clothing, walking back to the hangar with Lieutenant Adams. He breathed in the chilly spring air and felt his lungs expanding with some gratification. Had the enormity of his new task sunk in yet? Yes, it had. Yet it wasn't the harrowing experience he expected. At least, not yet. The joy of being alive was a little more intense. Perhaps a layer of dread in the background of his mind. He knew he was frightened and didn't want to do it. But something inside resigned him to what had to be done. He was more scared of trying to get out of it. There was no way he could find a credible reason to not go on the mission.

'You'll need that coat and boots. Gets bloody cold up there,' said Adams, trying to make small talk.

As they entered the hangar, Norris, Cooper and Tibbit stood up from the table where they were loading the thick drum magazines.

Cooper was still frowning as he spoke. 'Your Vickers gun is all primed and ready, sir. We're just on the last drums for the Lewis.'

'Good work, Cooper. As I'm sure you chaps have deduced, my new acting observer is going to be Maloney. We'll need to be ready in thirty-five minutes. All in cockpits, ready and waiting with Captain Polden's kite ready too.'

'The captain's kite is ready and waiting, sir. We prepared yours as you went to see the major, sir. We thought it best to assume you had a new observer,' Cooper answered.

'Excellent, let's do this final bit then, men. Our mission is still on schedule.'

CHOCKS AWAY

Norris was showing Tibbit where to put a small order of new spark plugs. He had opened a drawer, revealing a large number already in storage inside rectangular boxes of various brands.

'I never realised there were so many makes,' Tibbit mumbled, looking in the drawer.

'Mainly Lodge, KLG and Champion,' muttered Norris. 'They're just various colour boxes for different sized spark plugs. Look at the KLG range of plugs, all in their own colour box. Every one except for the particular size the KLG makes. And that's the one we want, bugger it.'

'There're some Igna and Hobson plugs too—' began Tibbit, as Norris stopped him mid-sentence.

'I know, Tibby, and this Hobson one is the right size. It will do. I just like this size in the KLG plug a little better.'

'Oh, why is that?' asked Tibbit, expecting to get the run-down on what spark plug was better.

'I think the KLG one has a better colour box,' replied Norris, grinning like a big kid.

'Oh,' Tibbit replied, then realised it was a pathetic answer. 'Hell's bells, you had me going then.' He couldn't help but chuckle. The recruit was rapidly coming to the conclusion that Norris and Cooper were a couple of rum characters. He also realised they enjoyed the odd joke at a new recruit's expense.

All three air mechanics giggled, having their little light-hearted moment. Cooper and Norris enjoyed Tibbit's amiable demeanour. Each could tell the new lad would fit in easily.

'Let's replace that spark plug with one our Cooper wants. He always seems to want one of the twelve cylinders touched up,' said Norris. 'I don't think there's anything wrong with the one already in place. However, if Cooper wants a pristine spark plug for that one cylinder, then he gets his way.'

'There's a slight sound difference on the cyl-inder that I mentioned earlier. Probably fine, but why take a chance?' Cooper lifted the cowling and looked inside at the immaculate engine. He took the necessary tool and removed one of the spark plugs before taking the new one from the box that Norris had given him. He quickly and firmly replaced it, then fastened the cowling back in place.

Norris winked at Tibbit, then said, 'Not worth taking any form of risk for one plug that takes seconds to replace.'

Tibbit sighed and nodded. 'Oh, I agree with you there.'

'Look what the cat's dragged in,' called Cooper.

Two more air mechanics came into the hangar to help Cooper, Norris and Tibbit. Each of them wore big cherub smiles. 'We've been sent in here to rough it with you blokes for a while,' grumbled one.

'God love us,' yelled Norris. 'It's Burke and Hare.'

'Afternoon, body snatchers,' added Cooper, ribbing the two smiling mechanics. It was obvious that Cooper and Norris were up for a minor lark and camaraderie.

'Who's this then?' asked one of the men jovially, nodding at Tibbit and smiling.

'This is the new lad,' Cooper replied. 'Greg "Tibby" Tibbit is the name. Tibby to his mates.'

'And only his best mates,' added Norris humorously. He turned to Tibbit and continued, 'These two lads are Billy O'Hare and Harry Burke.'

'Can we call you Tibby?' said Billy O'Hare, chuckling.

'Yeah, we'll be ya best mates, Tibby.' Harry Burke laughed.

Tibbit laughed too. 'Of course you can.'

'Well, I like the bloke already,' added O'Hare.

'Let's get to it then, me old body snatchers,' Cooper called.

'Yep.' O'Hare smiled, then looked to Air Mechanic Harry Burke. 'Let's help them take this big old bird outside.'

'Still carting off birds then,' Norris mocked the visitors.

'Carting off birds?' Tibbit responded.

'Burke and Hare used to do that for dissection back in the day,' Cooper replied knowledgeably.

O'Hare smiled. 'Wouldn't take much notice of your fellow mechanics, Tibby. They're never the sharpest knives in the drawer.' Tibbit just grinned and nodded compliantly. The historical joke was lost on him.

Burke also chuckled. 'If you're a good boy and eat all your greens at dinner time, I'm sure Cooper and Norris will tell you about the creepy tale for a nice little bedtime story.'

Tibbit shook his head and laughed, knowing there was banter in there somewhere. He accompanied the other four men around the first Bristol

F2B. They lifted the rear of Lieutenant Adams' plane and wheeled it forward out of the hangar. While they were performing the task, Maloney came out from the locker area in his long leather coat, leather flying cap and goggles. He instantly decided to help. The air mechanic duties were still with him, and he needed to be close to his friends.

'Well, just look at you, Dermot,' said Norris, trying to continue with the friendly banter, but his heart wasn't in it. All were concerned for his well-being.

The aircraft moved easily over the grass on its yellow plated wheels. Each man pushing the Bristol F2B the required distance in a very short space of time. When at the designated spot, the air mechanics put the end of the biplane to rest on the clear patch of grass. The afternoon was pleasant. A blue sky with scattered fluffy clouds. From another hangar two more Bristol F2Bs were being wheeled out.

'Look at that. Like clockwork,' Burke said.

'Put the chucks in place then, Harry.' O'Hare grinned.

'They're going on stage as a double act when this war is over,' Norris called to Tibbit, loud enough for all to hear.

'What, as Burke and Hare?' Tibbit looked confused.

'It's very catchy,' replied O'Hare, playing along with Norris and his banter.

'It certainly raises an eyebrow,' said Cooper sarcastically.

Burke and O'Hare put the yellow-painted wooden chocks against the wheels. Then all six air mechanics, including Acting Observer Maloney, returned to the canvas hangar for Captain Polden's aircraft. They repeated the same manoeuvre. Within less than ten minutes, both Bristol F2B biplanes were ready and waiting for their respective crews alongside the other two planes from the other hangar. Soon a gathering of air mechanics were awaiting their pilots and observers to appear.

'The pilots' kites are ready and waiting,' said Cooper. 'They're looking good,' said O'Hare.

'Here comes the Hucks,' called Burke.

Norris looked to Tibbit. 'Did ya see and hear that, Tibby? Our Burke and Hare are definitely a complete double act. They'll be touring all those seaside places to do shows. I think our Burke and Hare act should do well on stage.'

'Yes,' agreed Cooper. Then sarcastically added, 'Sweeping it.'

Harry Burke chuckled. 'Oh, did you hear that, Billy?'

'Pure jealousy,' O'Hare retorted. 'A couple of big girl's blouses who should shut up and get on with their knitting.'

Tibbit grinned at the playful camaraderie between the air mechanics and was sure he would enjoy the posting as long as he didn't learn too much in the way of Morse code and clock coding. As his new friends kept saying, 'Being ground maintenance is fine. Aircrew is a different kettle of fish.' And Tibbit could see no reason to doubt such advice.

From across the airfield, all made out the approach of the Hucks starter truck. The engine chugged away as the truck with its on-board apparatus rolled over the wet sod, the propeller pole swaying slightly despite being fixed down.

'This is all moving along very quickly. Is that long pole to the front the turner that fixes to the prop?' asked Tibbit.

'It is, Tibby. No standing on ceremony now, matey,' Norris replied.

'Our poor Maloney won't know what's hit him,' whispered Cooper anxiously. He looked over to Maloney, who was standing away from them, awaiting Lieutenant Adams to come out.

'Oh, I think the poor sod has a fair idea,' Norris replied with a sigh.

'Here comes Captain Polden and Cadet Observer Elliott.' Cooper stood to attention and saluted the captain. The others were a split second behind with their salutes.

Captain Polden smiled and returned the salute with Cadet Observer Elliott walking a few paces behind. Each man seemed comically dressed in leather flying caps with long leather coats complemented by their respective scarves and thick gloves. Both seemed in high spirits.

The two brief guest air mechanics, O'Hare and Burke, sauntered off back to their tent hangar a little way along from the waiting aircraft.

'Don't forget to write,' Norris called after them.

One of them might have replied with a colourful choice metaphor, but not in front of Captain Polden. They just ambled off with the looks of frustrated schoolboys that might get their revenge during a future playtime.

'You must be the new chap,' said Captain Polden, smiling at Tibbit. He was standing in his cockpit looking down. 'Don't get led astray by these two dodgy chaps, AM Tibbit.'

Norris and Cooper chuckled together and Tibbit realised that it was a slice of banter from the good-natured captain.

'I'll try not to, sir,' replied Tibbit.

This made Captain Polden laugh as he looked at his observer Elliott who also sniggered. Each man sat down into their respective cockpits. Elliott sat facing backwards looking towards the tail fin. He was doing a preliminary check of the Lewis gun and the inner rack containing the Lewis drum magazines.

'The camera is all set and ready, sir,' said Cooper to Cadet Observer Elliott.

'Thank you, AM Cooper, might get a snapshot of the Kaiser, aye?' replied Elliott, giving him a thumbs up.

'That'll make for a grand post card, sir.' Cooper grinned. He liked Cadet Observer Elliott.

'Here comes Lieutenant Adams,' said Tibbit nervously as he looked to Maloney.

'I feel like a duck out of water,' hissed Maloney.

For a moment, all went silent. Maloney fell in behind Lieutenant Adams as the officer climbed up on the wing and into his cockpit. The young Irishman turned back to his mechanic friends with a resigned smile. Then he clambered up and into the observer cockpit to sit backwards facing his tail fin. He proceeded to do the same thing as Elliott – check his Lewis gun was in order and the drum magazines. He looked up and smiled to Cooper and Norris when he saw the smaller empty forty-seven-round drum magazine – their little hoax magazine for their silly little disposable trick. One they had often discussed. None of them ever expected to use the lure, but now it seemed more like a good luck charm.

Maloney said something to Lieutenant Adams, who responded with a wave. After that, he turned his attention to the mechanics.

'Any problems we should bear in mind?' Adams smiled.

'None, sir. Everything is in order, sir. Your Biff is as good as she'll ever be,' said Cooper.

The two men went through the motions of buckling their harnesses. Adams to the front, with Maloney to the rear. Within moments, both Bristol F2B aircraft were ready and waiting, with pilots and observers eager to get on with the mission.

The Ford Model T Hucks starter came to a rumbling halt before the plane occupied by Lieutenant Adams and Maloney. Each man checked their harness straps a second time. Maloney looked at his two belts attached to either side of the airframe. He clipped each end to his right and left side. These straps allowed him to stand in the rear cockpit and use the Lewis gun and the camera. A little freedom of movement that Maloney didn't welcome but he understood the necessity.

The Hucks' driver stopped the truck but left the engine ticking over for a moment as he judged the short distance to the plane's propeller. Then he slowly and carefully edged the truck forward.

Cooper took the extended rod at the front of the on-board Hucks starter contraption. He carefully unfastened the holding bar and lifted the pole. He then attached it to the central bolt of the aircraft's propeller and looked back at the driver.

'Attached!' he called. Again, the driver stopped and pulled the handbrake, leaving the truck's engine ticking over.

Cooper walked away and stood to the flank, then called, 'Front fuel on.'

'Front fuel on,' repeated Lieutenant Adams.

'Throttle closed,' shouted Cooper.

'Throttle closed,' yelled Adams.

'Switches off,' Cooper continued.

'Switches off,' acknowledged Adams.

'Ready to prime!' Cooper called.

'Ready to prime,' yelled Adams as he opened the primer tap and pumped four shots into the engine that was being gently turned by the Hucks pole at the front propeller. Once this was done, Adams turned the primer off, calling out his moves to Cooper.

'Isolator closed.'

'Isolator closed,' repeated Cooper.

'Fully retarded,' shouted Adams.

'Fully retarded,' Cooper shouted to the Hucks' driver.

'Crack throttle set,' Adams called.

'Crack throttle set.' Cooper looked to the Hucks' driver again.

'Outside switches on,' Adams yelled again.

'Outside switches on,' Cooper repeated.

'Contact!' Adams sounded delighted.

'Contact,' screamed Cooper as the Hucks' driver beamed with schoolboyish delight.

The Hucks long propeller rod at the front vigorously kicked and twisted back into life, turning the prop with a stronger force. The aircraft engine roared as the whirling propellers went into swift motion. The blur of rotor blades as the Hucks truck unhooked from the central propeller bolt and backed away compliantly with its extension pole, putting the starter apparatus at a distance from the spinning fan blades.

'Chocks away!' The wheel stops were pulled from the front. Adams waved an all clear and moved the Bristol F2B gently forward. The Hucks truck reversed in an arc away from the aircraft's forward motion.

Maloney's heart leaped and his stomach churned. This was it! He shook nervously as the Bristol F2B moved forward onto the grass runway, rumbling along the turf as they increased their speed along the smooth section of grass. He was looking back at his receding air mechanic crew beyond the tail fin, knowing that his two close friends, Norris and Cooper, were trying to put on a brave face. The new man Tibbit looked concerned too. His two old friends had probably told the recruit about how dangerous going up in a Biff really was. All of them waved at the departing aircraft as it continued bumping along the grass runway. The desire to look down into his cockpit was immense. There was no need to look elsewhere as the tents and hedgerows passed by. Yet he felt compelled to. Perhaps he could put the Gosport system in place for communication with Lieutenant Adams. He inserted the speech and ear funnel hoses into their connectors, taking mere seconds. When he looked back out of the cockpit, tents and container sections passed by quicker. The engine was working up to a new rumbling crescendo. Maloney could feel it in every part of his body. Any moment now! Any moment soon!

Then came the sudden gentle rising of the tail fin as the Bristol F2B motored along quicker – running on the two wheels at the front under the carriage frame. A strange balancing act as Maloney's insides stirred a little more. Then the entire plane gently lifted into the air, the elevation coming much quicker than expected. Maloney was grateful for the saving wind-rush about his head. It was invigorating and helped to calm him while he adjusted his senses to the ground falling away from the plane. Suddenly, Maloney was feeling the uplifting sensation of flight. He looked over the cockpit and saw the ground moving further away from the Bristol F2B's steady climb. His reason began to falter. He resurrected the anxious feelings of dread and feared his heart might leap into his mouth. How long would this disturbing mindset last?

Would he eventually get it under control? How long before they got back? Would they get back?

'Can you hear me, Maloney?' said Lieutenant Adams, his voice buzzing over the intercom headset – their delicate Gosport system. Primitive yet adequate. And thankfully soothing.

'Yes, sir. Very clear. Can you hear me, sir?' Maloney tested his voice funnel as he looked back at the airfield they were leaving behind.

'Yes, Maloney. I can hear you clearly. So, our Gosport system is doing fine. Have you got your Morse transmitter and check code ready and waiting?' Adams sounded completely at ease which Maloney found very helpful. He was looking down at his various devices and was content that the Morse transmitter and check codes were ready and waiting.

'All in order, sir.'

'Very good,' replied Adams. 'Do a quick check on the Lewis and make sure your harness straps are secure before checking. I know you have already checked them, but do so again, old chap.'

The cold swirl of the spring air was whipping Maloney's face, and thankfully the goggles did much to protect his eyes. He was certain without such protectors, he would have had great trouble keeping his eyes open in such wind. He gingerly stood up. The panorama of the land falling away and stretching in all directions was magnificent. The blue sky, with its little fluffy clouds, received more attention from him than usual. He looked over the starboard side and marvelled at the expansive patchwork of green fields – different shades of dark and light green – and the light colour of the roads – a network of veins with uneven blobs of big clusters of woodlands scattered here and there. He also made out another Bristol F2B following them.

Maloney pulled the lock that looked like a bicycle brake up against the Scarff ring mount. It was just beneath the Lewis gun. With ease, the crossbar rose via the side spokes with the gun attached upon the central bar. This was an easy move, and Maloney had worked the device often during maintenance. Now it was for real. He turned the Scarff ring with complete ease to port, pointing the Lewis gun upwards towards the blue and the gently floating fleet of fluffy clouds. He released the brake grip, allowing the gun to lock into the spoked teeth. The swivel mount was sturdy. It was pleasing to see that everything was in order considering he had done the maintenance personally. Sighing, he looked down at the empty forty-seven-round good luck drum in the storage rack. It was alongside the full ninety-seven-round drums. Cooper and Norris had remembered the best of luck ploy – should it be needed. He smiled to himself. Odd little super-stitions that men liked to abide by. A small smile creased his face amid the lashing squall. How glad he was of the long coat and the thigh-high sheep-skin boots to keep out the thrashing bluster. Now such garments were deeply appreciated.

'The Lewis seems fine, sir,' Maloney called back through the voice funnel.

'Give it a short three or four bursts, please, Maloney? Just to be on the safe side,' the lieuten-ant's voice called back through the earmuffs.

'Will do, sir. I'm pointing upwards and to port.'

Maloney licked his lips and used the outer cir-cumference of the wider sight, just where the hori-zontal bar touched the outer rim. He understood the gun-sight firing ahead of the centre circle sight to adjust for target movement along the port or star-board sides. He imagined there was an enemy air-craft out there on the port side. Where the outer rim connected to the central bar, the radial bar going back to the centre point, he would be firing in front of an imagined moving trajectory. The time lapse would adjust for the oncoming target to fly into the projectile's path. Easy in theory, but in practice it meant judging the distance and speed correctly against bullet velocity. It remained crude guesswork but roughly shots in the right direction. 'I can see

Captain Polden is far back and approaching from the starboard side.' Maloney pulled the bolt to the rear and let it lock. Then he squeezed the trigger for a short four-round burst. The pan mag turned with each pa, pa, pa, pa as four shell cases fell out one by one. One shell had a tracer which delighted Maloney as he saw the bullet's path appear to arc slightly.

All seemed well, and he heard Adams' voice in his earmuffs call contentedly, 'That all sounds in order.'

'It is, sir. The Lewis seems very sound.' He realised the lieutenant could see him in the rear-view mirror and hoped he couldn't hear his pounding heart. Maloney judged his anxiety was up and holding steady at just below frightened senseless on an imagined circular-faced fear meter. The panoramic land was beautiful with all its tiny meadows, woodlands and roads. How he longed to walk among the fields right now.

As he looked out over the tail fin, he saw the accelerating climb and approach of the other Bristol F2B.

'I see Captain Polden is rapidly catching up.' Adams sounded pleased by the fact. He noted other Bristol formations to the starboard as well. Another two groups each consisting of a pair.

Maloney could make out Captain Polden and Cadet Observer Elliott. 'We have them coming along the starboard, sir.'

'Very good, Maloney. Keep an eye out for anything else coming from the rear. We're expecting two squadrons of Sopwith Camels.'

'Will do, sir.'

Maloney was beginning to calm even though the height was very unsettling. He was transfixed by the various shades of green fields, marvelling at the vast expanse of roads and land in all directions. As they climbed higher, he drank in the gorgeous blue sky and the sight of wispy clouds below, obscuring some of the fields and villages.

'We're above clouds, sir,' muttered Maloney in awe.

'Indeed, Maloney. I'm forgetting this is your first time. Some clouds are now below us, albeit very thin hazy little things.'

'There's something coming closer on the port rear, sir,' Maloney said nervously.

'Can you see them clearly yet, Maloney?'

He pulled up his voice hose and called, 'Some specks to my right rear of the tail fins, sir. Very distant like a small swarm of gnats coming towards us. I can't make them out, but they're coming from our patch.'

'I've got them,' Adams replied, looking in his rear-view mirror. 'Relax, Maloney. They're our chaps in their Sopwith Camels.'

'Another group of aircraft approaching at our level. Again on the port rear, sir.' Maloney wasn't sure if he'd said that right. He was an observer without certain aspects of training.

'Got them, Maloney. More of our Sopwith chaps. Fine fellows in a scrap. They'll be falling in alongside and all around us very soon.'

Adams looked across his immediate starboard side to where Captain Polden had settled a little above them. He swivelled his plane and then made hand signals, which Captain Polden acknowledged with a thumbs up.

Maloney surmised that Lieutenant Adams was letting him know that more friendly aircraft were approaching.

As the Sopwith Camel aircraft fell into position all around the Bristol F2B aircraft, Maloney felt a little more settled. Another two Bristol F2Bs also fell in with the group of Allied planes as they made their way towards the front lines.

'We're getting close to the front, Maloney. Can you hear the guns?'

Maloney briefly removed his earmuffs and listened. The unmistakeable sound of artillery firing came from ahead and below. Then he quickly replaced his covers and spoke into his voice funnel.

'Those guns deliver a rather unwelcome welcome, sir.'

Adams laughed. 'Indeed, Maloney. I like that. An "unwelcome welcome" is exactly what that sound is.'

Maloney looked down through cloud gaps to where the approaching lines of tortured earth gradually came towards them. The lush green meadows and woodlands were replaced by a great winding serpent of destruction from north to south. A line of broken and twisted pockmarked craters – a terrain that looked sterile and abhorrent compared to what he had looked down upon just moments earlier.

'There you see it, Maloney.' Adams sighed over the Gosport system. 'The consequence of man's inhumanity towards all and everything when competing for victory.'

'It makes me wonder, sir. Have we reached a peak in our ability to destroy? I can't imagine anything worse than this.' Maloney was dumbstruck as he peered down towards the horrid and winding trenches.

Adams' voice came direct through the Gosport, playing down the battering airstream. 'Trust me, Maloney. Men will find ever newer and more terrible ways of destroying one another. War is still evolving even now. Look at hypocrites like us in this aircraft flying above the killing grounds. Who would ever have thought of this a few years ago?'

Maloney gingerly lowered himself down on his cockpit seat. He was thinking about what Lieutenant Adams had said. Here he was in a war and up in the sky. As a child, he could never have dreamed of such a thing. And trenches below filled with combatant men stretching for hundreds of miles. The scale of the war was colossal. No big armies marching in formations, lines of rifle men making their stand, firing fusillades at an advancing line of enemy soldiers. Everything had changed. All was a stalemate. Everything was one final push. An eternity of final pushes. He finally muttered into the voice pipe, 'Can it ever end? Will it ever end?'

There was no reply. The squadron of planes climbed higher into the blue and seemed to do this for some time before Adams' voice came through the ear flap receivers. 'It certainly won't be ending yet, Maloney. We'll be going through a section of ground flak when we cross over the German lines. That will be any moment now. This can be a little anxious for a first timer. Get ready for some impressive flak.'

'Will do, sir,' Maloney replied nervously. He looked to starboard where Captain Polden and Cadet Observer Elliott were in their Bristol F2B flying alongside. No doubt charged with an enemy gun emplacement to direct artillery fire towards. Elliott smiled back at Maloney and waved his gloved hand. Maloney complied with an acknowledging return wave. He then turned to his port side and spotted the young pilot of a Sopwith Camel single fighter. The lone pilot looked over, as though alerted by some sixth sense. He gave Maloney a comrade's wave too. Again, Maloney acknowledged with a wave back. He looked over the single-seater biplane, noting the olive-green fuselage and British insignia – a thin white circumference with an inner thick blue circle to an inner white circle and the red centre spot. There was the letter C in white next to the insignia and then the light grey colour around the engine casing to the front. As his eye ran over the forward section, he noted the twin synchronised Vickers machine guns before the pilot, each timed to fire through the propellers. The young pilot looked quietly confident with a grimly set jaw as though this young man had been on other missions and knew the way of things. No longer a fledgling, but a veteran. Someone of invaluable experience. Maloney wondered how many kills the young pilot had made.

'Going over no man's land now.' Adams' voice broke through his thoughts. Maloney couldn't resist another look down through the wispy clouds, despite the anxiety it brought.

He gasped at the sight. The horrid craters that pockmarked the earth looked more intense directly below. Nothing but scarred and tortured land. Total devastation – complete corruption. Then he noted the very visible trench lines of the enemy and saw wretched life. Tiny ant-like human beings moving along the conduits of trench works.

Little human termites devouring the land, thought Maloney, spellbound by the sight, his fear receding before the vile wonder of what was below.

Then the first explosions of flak began. Maloney almost jumped out of the observer's cockpit. He had been warned, but it still took him by surprise. Dark grey puffs of explosive smoke spreading more shrapnel about in all directions. These outbursts were initially below the squadron, but the second wave of flak quickly exploded around their level of flight.

One explosion was just to the rear of the fin and seemed to fall away from their Biff's flight path. Another few feet or a moment earlier and it might have smashed through the undercarriage. The retreating grey smoky tendrils unnerved Maloney as he looked at the cloth fabric about the plane. It would do little to prevent shrapnel ripping through it. His heart raced, and the helplessness of his situation gnawed at him. He gulped anxiously and staggered back down in his seat, gripping the rim of his cockpit and the Scarff ring bars. His eyes bulged with fear as he bit his bottom lip. The scattered explosions and the sporadic shrapnel were appearing all about them. This was hair-raising terror upon a scale he could never imagine. The cold sweat of dread ran down his back while he battled with his inner self to try and show some composure.

He glanced at the leather sleeves of his coat and knew the skin beneath was under the onslaught of tingling sensations. Uproars that made the hairs stand on end. Certain that the sweat and stiffened hairs would seep through his garments – even his thick airman's coat.

There was also the sudden shaking from shock-waves – the turbulence as the horrid explosive billows continued erupting about them. If one such blasting surge was close enough, it would be unthinkable. If they continued, the odds against them would increase – the mathematical probability was there. What damage might be caused by a burst close to such rickety contraptions and their flimsy canvas covering? The whole squadron appeared to be much more vulnerable. Maloney knew where every nut and bolt was, even the ones that were essential to keeping their kite airborne. The continued turbulence caused him to think of nuts and bolts rattling loose and the entire aircraft falling apart at such altitude. He gritted his teeth, desperate to contain his strained wits.

'My word,' muttered Lieutenant Adams' voice. 'The Hun seems to have gauged the correct height and very quickly.'

'That doesn't sound very comforting, sir,' replied Maloney half-jokingly, yet still scared stiff.

More dark explosive clouds were rising to their starboard and to port. Horrid booms – more smoky eruptions, more grey tendrils following the scattered shrapnel's path. A few more to the rear of the fin as Maloney's mouth dropped open in further dreaded awe. Some dark grey outbursts of smoke were a little low, others a little high. Maybe the bursts were too far away to cause damage? But it only needed one to explode close to them. Perhaps it was the noise of each boom that caused the greater alarm. He tried to convince himself that it was just a boom and nothing else that could unnerve him.

Still not likely to happen, Maloney thought, needing to convince himself that such was so.

He was steadying himself when a blast of grey smoke erupted beneath the wheels of the Sopwith Camel to the port side. The very plane he'd been studying and whose pilot had waved to him moments before. Now, the outburst of the flak's flumes spread in many directions like a demented grey starfish. One such smoking tendril had smashed up through the wheel mounts and undercarriage of the Sopwith Camel fighter with the tearing sound of the fuselage canvas. The lower engine casing burst into flames beneath the aircraft. The sudden look on the young man's petrified face as he struggled to shut certain fuel feeds off. Despite his best efforts, the doomed pilot could not see the burning wake beneath his plane. There was nothing Maloney could do, and he knew very clearly that the ill-fated airman was beyond help.

For a serene moment, the condemned pilot looked at other aircraft around him as though someone could help in some unexplainable way. But the torrid flames beneath his plane meant that miracles were nowhere in sight. The billowing black smoke spewed away angrily, leaving the sight of the woeful pilot trying to maintain his burning aircraft for a few moments longer. Just a few more feet with his comrades – flying along with his squadron for another moment. He even managed a momentary smile as though he had the Sopwith Camel under control and the wake of black smoke might be ignored. Say nothing and it might go away. Alas, the engine spluttered. Reluctant to continue with the pathetic pretence, the pilot looked about again, fear devouring his cringing face. A face that knew no one could help him. His expression twisted into the look of a terrified little boy for a split second and then became firm again. The condemned pilot looked across at Maloney as the fire below continued to belch out plumes of black smoke trailing out in an expanding wake. The young man half-heartedly smiled again for a split second.

Maloney gulped and forced himself watch the final hopeless moment as the Sopwith Camel's young pilot went down, struggling with the spade stick. This time, the doomed pilot's face was no longer visible. It couldn't torture him anymore. The fear and despair were gone, falling with the burning plane that was suddenly veering down and arcing away from the formation. The engine screamed in protest and left the squadron to continue with the mission. The flak had ended as quickly as it started, but the enemy had scored one hit.

Maloney couldn't rid himself of the horrific memory. The diabolical stages of panic, resolve, bravery and acceptance in the wretched pilot's face. His limbs grappling with redundant controls. Was that what it was like? All that remained was the diminishing, whirring engine, its whining scream becoming fainter with the burning aircraft's descent. The thick trail of bulging black smoke would soon disperse, and the pilot would fade from memory. The condemned young man was gone with the protesting and burning biplane. No one seemed concerned anymore. Out of sight and out of mind. Maloney remained transfixed. He couldn't get over the horror of the pilot's dreadful demise.

'All that time to think while falling,' Maloney whispered to himself, knowing the pilot would be twisting and turning, strapped into a contraption of fire that was falling from the sky. He couldn't help but stare morbidly down. Thankfully, he could no longer see anything. In the end, nothing was left to feed the contradiction of his wicked and serene fixations. The screaming engine had gone silent, and the lieutenant's voice could be heard in his ears via the Gosport system.

'Keep an eye out for the enemy aircraft now that we're past the flak, Maloney, there's a sound fellow. We're getting close to the observation target site. First the Morse code transmitter for our artillery units to begin firing. Then you can check the hits to the clock code before transmitting back.'

'Yes, sir. Making ready,' Maloney replied as he got back into the cockpit and organised his checks. He prepared to send the first Morse signal for his artillery unit to commence firing.

'Ready to send when target is reached, sir.' He wanted to witness the first trial shots once they had seen their target. But first they had to get there. All had settled again as the squadron pressed on to their various mission destinations.

'So far, the cost is one Sopwith Camel to ground fire,' said Adams soberly.

'Was that a lucky shot, sir?' asked Maloney.

'I suppose it was for the Hun, old boy. Not for the poor chap in the plane. God rest his soul.'

'Yes, sir. God rest his soul.'

'Not over yet, Maloney. I'm afraid that was a mere hors d'oeuvre. The main course is yet to come.'

'What's hors d'oeuvre, sir?' Maloney was confused.

'It's what us upper-crust posh people serve as an appetiser. A small starter before the main course of a meal which is a bigger dish altogether.' Adams laughed.

'Meaning there's more to come,' replied Maloney. 'I thought as much, sir. I'm not feeling very hungry at the moment. Though I've always wanted to go to one of the upper-crust posh dinners.'

Adams chuckled. Maloney had a good sense of humour. Better to let that out with the festering fear.

'I think our target is ahead, Maloney. I can see those big buildings from Major Laws' photo map. Argh, yes! And that crater. Can you send the Morse to the artillery unit to commence their firing? We can then do the necessary checks against our chaps' shots.'

'I've just sent it, sir,' Maloney said, repeating the signal for good measure.

'That shell fire is certainly receding as we get deeper behind the enemy lines,' muttered Adams through his voice hose.

'It's become a minor humdrum noise,' Maloney agreed as they flew over a less scarred area. 'We've still got to go back that way yet.'

Adams chuckled. 'We might be fighting our way back among the Hun flying circus. The ground fire won't happen as either side will fear hitting their own planes.'

'I can't hear any sound of a shell coming this way from the lines. I hope our lads got the message.' Maloney looked for the target area.

'That's due to the close sound of our engines and the height of our Biff. Plus, we have our earphones in.' Adams sniggered. 'You'll see something—'

Just then, an eruption of mud and flame exploded close to a netted crater, a long way down but very visible. It took Maloney by surprise.

'There she goes,' yelled Adams.

'The shell has landed in the C section of the clock code, sir. Just away from the crater. The Hun artillery is below that netting, I presume,' Maloney called back, watching the muddy puff of flame and then smoke.

'What's your estimate? Mine is C at two o'clock.'

'Snap! That's what I call too, sir. C section at two o'clock. I'll send that now,' Maloney called into the voice hose.

'Splendid,' agreed Adams. 'Let's see what our chaps send back this time.'

Instantly, Maloney signalled back to the unknown artillery position. Lieutenant Adams circled the entire area around the crater with a few of the Sopwith Camels patrolling above. Suddenly more anti-aircraft guns kicked into life and more flak explosions were erupting about them.

'Not as intense this time, Maloney,' said Adams reassuringly.

'The shots seem way out of line if they're aiming at us, sir,' Maloney agreed. His interest was concentrated upon the great German gun under the netting in the crater.

A second explosion erupted on the ground below. Another shell from their own British artillery unit, trying to fix in on the enemy gun.

'Well, that was a close guess adjustment. It's gone across to the other side of the crater but closer to the Hun's big old girl,' yelled Adams, seeming a little more confident of the unseen artillery unit hitting the enemy gun emplacement. 'You called a good reading there, Maloney.'

'That was B at seven o'clock,' yelled Maloney into the voice hose.

Adams' voice came back, 'Good call, Maloney, send it on.'

Maloney began the Morse sequence again and waited for the next adjusted shot. He stood and leaned slightly over and looked down from his rear observer cockpit. His face wrinkled against the wind, but his vision was clear through the flying goggles. His scarf flapping in the intense breeze. The fear of height was gone. His concentration was on the enemy big gun hidden within the net-covered crater. He marvelled at the sight through the net.

'Good God, sir! I can see little human ants struggling along with a stretcher-like thing, so I can.' Once again, Maloney was intrigued.

Adams called back, 'No doubt carrying heavy shells to their big old girl of a gun. They'll be slinging that heavy thing back at our chaps' lines. The very lines our squadron has recently flown over.'

The flak was growing a little more intense and Adams took the Bristol F2B up a little higher as he continued to circle the target area. The guarding Sopwith Camels were doing the same. Maloney reached for his binoculars by the drum magazines. The view of the crater with the camouflaged netting was much better. The enemy artillery men were clearer too, though they jostled in and out of focus due to the plane's turbulence.

'I can clearly make out the Hun barrel beneath the netting, sir,' Maloney yelled into his voice pipe. 'That Hun artillery piece is a big old bird, that's for sure.'

At that precise moment, a shell struck the netting. Maloney didn't hear a projectile coming across. The explosion just happened.

Even though he was expecting it, the sudden upsurge of fire and earth took him by surprise yet again.

'My God! That was horrendous.' Maloney looked down in awe. He had never witnessed anything like it.

'Good Lord! That is a devilishly big bang down there.'

'Oh aye, it's a hit, sir!' Maloney yelled. 'To be sure, that was one hell of a strike.'

A great plume of debris and fire continued to climb and spread outwards. Maloney was aghast as he looked down at the wicked eruption, knowing the violent explosion couldn't climb and reach them at such a height. Where the crater and netting had been with its ant men clamouring around the big gun, there was just the climbing debris of fire and soil.

'Splendid, Maloney. Let the lads know they have the range – spot on.'

Maloney was already sitting down and hunched forward to avoid the whipping airstream. He was in the process of sending the Morse code, informing the unknown artillery unit of their on-target strike. A second shell hit the enemy gun emplacement. The entire crater ignited again. A new ball of outspreading flame, a surge of more broken earth shooting outwards and upwards amid the expanding orange ball. For a moment, Adams and Maloney thought the second upsurge might reach them. But, thankfully, it stopped well below and cascaded back down. As the debris cleared, Maloney couldn't make out any part of the artillery piece or the netting. The little ant men were gone too. Perhaps everything was buried by the cascading soil as it returned to earth. There were now two craters looking like giant binocular lenses. Lenses that stared back up at them through the dissolving dust.

'Good God! They must have hit the shell storage facility,' called Adams delightedly. 'Right, let's climb and get some real good photographs for the major, shall we.' Adams laughed, his adrenalin flowing.

'Yes, sir,' Maloney replied, the vibe of gratification overwhelming all of his previous fears. How long would this last? This was a great mission achievement for Adams and Maloney in their Biff.

'Success by any stretch of expectation,' called Adams gratifyingly. 'A direct hit after just two clock code corrections is a stroke of luck for us.'

BACK AT THE HANGAR

The air mechanics were loading supplies on various shelves. Other parts were stored inside the sliding metal drawers of the cabinets. Each drawer was marked with a note informing of the contents. All the mechanics wanted to do something. None of them liked the idea of Maloney going out on the flights. Was this to be the shape of things to come for their colleague and friend Maloney?

'Our Dermot shouldn't be doing this,' muttered Norris. 'He's one of us – ground crew – and shouldn't be among the blooming observers. I thought they'd stopped this sort of thing last year. There seemed to be a drive for getting cadet observers trained. Young officer material and from the right type of background.'

'There is a certain snobbery about the aircrew,' began Cooper. 'What with being officers and coming from the right background and all. Yet as this war has progressed, the top brass do like to delve down into the ranks to pick out people from the humbler backgrounds.'

'The snobbery has gone right out of it. Especially where observers are concerned.' Norris was in agreement. 'But let's be honest, Cooper, we've even heard of pilots being taken from among air mechanics.'

'Yes, but I think they have to be observers first. I could be wrong, but I think they do the observer things to get started,' added Cooper, a little wary of Norris's vexed mood.

'So, our Dermot might end up piloting his own Biff next?' Norris spat disapprovingly. 'You must know he wouldn't want that. Not for all the tea in China.'

Cooper and Tibbit remained quiet. The new recruit had only been among them for a few hours, but he felt at one with the other two air mechanics, understanding their concern for Dermot Maloney. Nonetheless, Tibbit didn't know what to say that might console Norris. There were no plausible words that might settle the man.

'You know, the top brass have better cabinets than this,' said Cooper, completely changing the subject as he slammed the old metal drawer shut with considerable force. He wanted to think about anything and everything except for Dermot Maloney and the peril he would be in from now on. He closed the subject in his own way.

'Do they?' asked Tibbit naively. 'Why should an officer's cabinet be different from these?' he said, looking at all the metal cabinet drawers.

'Cooper means they have drinks cabinets.' Norris chuckled, happily moving on to the new topic of conversation. 'That always gets our Cooper's gander up. Top brass officers' drinks cabinets are a real ache for our Cooper. Isn't that so?'

'That's right,' Cooper agreed irately. 'And I bet they are made of some of the finest wood. Oak, mahogany – you name it, and a toff probably has it. Gets a soppy bunch of gits like us to carry the cabinet about for him. An entourage of drinks cabinets moving here and there.'

'I'm sure such officers don't bring oak or mahogany drinks cabinets to the front,' replied Tibbit, perplexed.

'The top brass do,' said Norris, quick to make such things known to the recruit. 'Your top brass cling to a drinks cabinet. Not your low-grade officers. I mean your top-notch as in, top brass. Our Major Laws is probably just one below the drinks cabinet blokes. It's once you get to Lieutenant-Colonel Wing Commander and up.'

Cooper laughed. 'Yeah. That's about it, Norris. One up to Brigadier-General or Major-General.'

'Therefore? Major Laws will be looking at a stylish drinks cabinet soon. Wing, brigade and division commanders do love a drinks cabinet.'

Tibbit frowned. 'I was in Major Laws' office before coming here. He had metal filing cabinets, and so do his personnel outside in the lobby. They're just the same as the ones we have.'

'Compared to the top brass, our...' Cooper looked around, making sure no officers were about before continuing. 'Major Laws is a toilet boy. A high-ranking toilet boy but not in the top brass league yet.'

'At least one more rank to go before being among the top brass,' added Norris. 'That's when he'll have a good old wooden drinks cabinet in his office.'

'All high up and fancy,' agreed Cooper.

Tibbit frowned at the two grinning air mechanics then laughed. 'You two are pulling my leg.'

Instantly, the smirks on Cooper's and Norris's faces were lost and their expressions became serious.

'Not at all, Tibby.' Cooper frowned. 'We're not like that,' added Norris.

Tibbit frowned, looking for the telltale sign of glee. But he couldn't spot anything. 'I think you two blokes are a bunch of wind-up merchants.'

Norris didn't flinch and gave nothing away. He looked up thoughtfully – like a wise old sage – and then continued. 'I've heard Field Marshal Kitchener had a beautiful drinks cabinet moved aboard HMS *Hampshire*. Evidently, he took this lovely piece of furniture wherever he went.'

'Oh yes,' agreed Cooper. 'I heard about his particular drinks cabinet. It was blooming legendary was that.'

'Get lost!' Tibbit chuckled. 'What a load of old toffee.'

Norris shook his head with a serious expression on his face. 'I'm telling you, Tibby. Our Field Marshal Kitchener loved his cabinet and had it taken aboard HMS *Hampshire* with him.'

'Well, that did him a fat lot of good, didn't it?' Tibbit was unsure whether to be shocked by the small talk or tell his two friends to get lost. He was sure that they were joking at first, but now they looked very serious. Or at least they seemed to be. 'HMS *Hampshire* was sunk with Earl Kitchener on board. He went down with the ship.'

'Yes, but his blooming drinks cabinet went with him. Which goes to show that wherever the top brass goes, so does his blooming drinks cabinet.' Cooper smiled satisfactorily.

'Do you think he took it upstairs or downstairs with him?' asked Norris, matter of fact.

Tibbit was shocked at the disrespect. 'I can't believe this conversation. He was one of our greatest field marshals. We should show some respect. You blokes sound like a couple of old biddies in a knitting group.'

'I think our Kitchener was overrated,' replied Norris.

'He was no Wellington, that's for sure,' Cooper agreed.

'The man has been dead for the last two years,' said Tibbit. 'His picture got thousands to join up. You know the advert – "Your Country Needs You".'

'And our lads certainly responded. A shepherd leading lambs to the slaughter, Tibby. There are many who think Earl Kitchener has a lot to answer for.' Cooper twitched his nose before scratching it.

'Led a lot of poor sods to their deaths. Wouldn't be surprised if the Froggies had the same thing too,' Norris said.

'Even the Hun,' agreed Cooper.

'Hold up,' moaned Tibbit. 'Is he Field Marshal or Earl Kitchener?'

'I think you'll find he qualifies as both,' replied Cooper.

Tibbit sighed. 'Well, whatever, our Kitchener was as much a man of circumstance as any of us. Someone who had to make decisions. Whatever course he chose would result in the consequence of men getting killed. There is no way around the problem. It's a rum deal for everyone and our Kitchener never got off scot-free when he boarded that fated ship. He's now among those casualties of war.'

Cooper sat there looking at Tibbit with one raised eyebrow. Despite the seriousness on his face, there was a touch of humour. 'I still think he may have gone downstairs as opposed to up.'

'Ah, you sods!' Tibbit laughed. 'You are winding me up, aren't you? The pair of you are trying to get my gander up.'

'We almost had him, Cooper. Did you see that?' Norris chuckled.

'For one little moment there, I thought he was going to bust a gut.' Cooper sniggered in agreement.

'Blooming easy on the squeezers – you nightmare geezers,' Tibbit remonstrated, trying not to laugh.

Cooper and Norris laughed at the recruit's words. 'He's got a language of his own,' said Norris, giggling.

Their mirth was infectious and Tibbit laughed along with them. It eased the tension and worry for their friend who was out on a flight mission. After a short time, the laughter subsided. The brief camaraderie of the moment was gratefully accepted by all.

'You do seem like a likely lad,' said Cooper. 'You should be fine here, mate.'

'I think we would be better off talking about Dermot Maloney,' said Norris, returning to more serious matters. 'Perhaps the subject is better than any high-ranking officer's drinks cabinet?' He looked at Tibbit and smiled before continuing, 'I'm not disrespecting the earl and saying he's not worth our consideration, Tibby. Just his blithering drinks cabinet.'

Cooper pursed his lips as though deep in thought. 'I think our Norris might have a point. Maloney is more worthy of consideration than a top brass man's drinks cabinet.'

'Alright then,' Norris acknowledged with another smile. 'What do you want to gripe about, Tibby? Let us have it. Cooper and I are all lugholes, matey.'

'How do you think it's going for Dermot?' asked Tibbit. 'Probably fine for this first mission,' replied Norris.

'Most first missions go well,' agreed Cooper. 'By that, I mean they tend to come back more often than not. It's when they keep going out, day in and day out. Sooner or later your luck is going to run out.'

'And you think Dermot is really on that road?' asked Tibbit.

'Of course, we do,' said Norris. 'That's why we're concerned, Tibby. Or have you not noticed?'

Tibbit sighed. 'You know, it is funny how these things go. There was a time four years ago that I remember well back when all this started. Men lining up in droves to enlist. And then as time went on, the enthusiasm seemed to settle. I don't think people are eager to throw the tail in, but it has become a chore that we must do. No one is as eager to get out here nowadays. It's just a resignation to a duty that calls. Blokes have to do their bit. No more blind patriotism but a patriotism that's resigned to the task.'

Cooper smiled at the young recruit. 'We can all remember those heady days back at the start, Tibby. We all believed we might teach the Hun a blooming good lesson. That never happened. Everyone on both sides of this war is getting an education, or at least a blooming rude awakening.'

'Were your parents happy, Tibby? When they found out you were in the air force as a mechanic and away from the front lines?' Norris asked. 'After all, this is a good area to do active service.'

'I presume you mean good, provided I don't show too much enthusiasm like Dermot did?' Tibbit smiled. 'As for being an air mechanic 3rd class, I don't think my mother or father knew what such a thing was. They understand there are aircraft and they've seen Zeppelin raids over Southend-on-Sea. I think they were scared of these things. My mother kept asking me if I was going up in the Zeppelins, bless her. My old dad didn't say too much, but I could see he was worried.'

'As long as we can stick this out, I mean by working on the aircraft in the hangar, then I think we stand a good chance of making it to the end of this madness,' said Cooper.

'On a ship or on the front as a soldier, there's a greater probability of stopping one,' agreed Norris.

'And our main danger here is learning too much beyond the aircraft maintenance,' added Tibbit with a touch of irritation. 'Trust me, fellas, you have really hammered that advice home and I can see clearly what has happened to Dermot. I've looked and learned within the first few hours of being here.'

Norris sniffed. 'There are some blokes who've been on the air mechanics since the start of this blooming caper. That Welsh bloke, Morris, in the number 2 hangar. Tends to keep himself to himself most of the time. But every now and then, you can get a good conversation out of him. Especially if you ask him about the early days of the air conflicts. They used to go up in the Avro 504 planes to do reconnaissance at first.'

'They use them on the training ground today. Much of our mechanics learning was with Avro 504s. There seems to be a lot of them.' Tibbit scratched his head, recollecting the training barracks.

'The best use for them now,' replied Cooper. 'They were quickly outdated. Even our Morris says that when harking on about the early stages of the air war. Strange saying that, it was only four years ago.'

Norris nodded his agreement. 'Morris says our pilots used to wave at the Hun planes coming over our lines. They would pass one another by and simply wave. All very toffy-nosed a few years back.'

'Who started shooting first?' Tibbit raised an eyebrow.

'No one knows for sure,' replied Cooper. 'But someone had to. Morris says that the Avro had the observer in the front and under the wing canopy. The pilot was at the rear and more exposed to the elements. Things were only just beginning to adapt. The observer might have had a rifle and the pilot a revolver. That's how it started at first.'

'Then some clever sod brought a machine gun.' Norris laughed. 'Everyone in the RFC was up in arms about the dishonour of it all.'

Cooper chuckled at the irony. 'Anyone would have thought it was a tickling competition.'

'Cooper is bang on the money, Tibby.' Norris grinned, displaying an array of tobacco-stained teeth. 'Take our respective armies. Hun, Froggie and our Tommies. They all thought the aircrew were a bunch of lounge lizards going out on solo flights to take photos, then back to relax in a nice mess hall. One that's stationed well behind the lines. There the pilots sit with a whiskey and splash plus a choice of cigar.'

'Don't they do that then?' Tibbit knew there was an officers' mess for the aircrew.

'Yes, knowing any day might be their last,' Cooper answered. 'But back then, I don't think the fear of being shot down was so strong. By the time the first year was over, the stress element came into it with more force.'

'Especially when they all stopped waving and started taking pot-shots at one another.' Norris agreed with his friend. 'That's when the whiskey and splashes became doubles and the flow of them was a little more excessive. Live for the moment and drink to forget. The aircrews learned to handle things in their own way.'

Tibbit rubbed the back of his neck. 'That puts us in a place where we are away from the lines and that's good. But we're watching these poor sods doing all the risk-taking. I'm planning to be a good mechanic for these airmen. If I can do something to help any pilot's kite, I'll be only too pleased.'

'That is wise, Tibby,' said Cooper as he heated the kettle over the stove. Another cup of tea would be on the way. 'I wonder how our newly appointed Acting Observer Dermot Maloney is doing right at this moment?'

FURTHER PARTS OF THE MISSION

'Do you have those little beauties in sight, Maloney?' Adams asked, peering down while steering the plane. He was in a very positive mood. The gun emplacement was gone and now they were photographing activity above a train station. Something he thought would be of great interest to Major Laws.

'I'm getting it all, sir.' Maloney changed the slides again for another photo shot. He held the rectangular-shaped camera with both hands and looked down through it, pressing the frame against the lip of the cockpit to keep it steady. 'There seems to be a lot of troop movements and new artillery pieces on the train.'

'Get as much as you can, Maloney. The Hun will be a little sore at us chaps intruding on their little party preparations,' added Adams.

The lieutenant took the Bristol F2B around the rail station scene again. The altitude was high, but the view of the enemy train station below was clear. So too were the train carriages. Maloney could also make out the little specks of people moving about. The whole place was a hive of activity.

Adams' voice came over the hose connector and into the ear plugs. 'Get what you can, old chap. Sooner or later, the enemy squadrons will seek us out. Anytime now. That's when the battle to return home will ensue.'

Maloney gulped back the dread while taking another photo shot. He knew the attempted return would be a traumatic event. A battle to get back in one piece. He had heard the stories from many pilots. For now, he wanted to remain focused on the immediate task before them. It would be best to leave it that way. As the acting observer, he would remain concentrating on the photographic part of his mission for as long as he could.

There was the usual flak exploding sporadically below them as they circled the scene. Puffs of distant smoke. Way off target. The barrage was too low to hinder their flight path or make them deviate in any way. Maloney continued to change slides and get as many photo shots as possible. He could imagine the major adding the new images to his already intense photographic map. No doubt there would be other photo opportunities in other areas.

'Coming in from the sun!' yelled Adams.

Maloney quickly put the camera device back inside his cockpit, knowing that the photo session was now as complete as it could be. He heard the howling dive before he saw the enemy. A slate-speckled Fokker DR1 triplane with patched tile patterns of grey, green, black and white. Its two Spandau machine guns clattered away at one of the Sopwith Camel escorts. The British biplane quickly and skilfully veered away from the attacking enemy aircraft. The wicked cat was among them, and the British planes were now the scattering pigeons.

Adams routinely and instantly took his Bristol F2B upwards at a steep climb. The Falcon-powered engine growled in anger as the plane swiftly charged to meet their protagonists head on, upwards and towards the growing buzz of diving enemy aircraft.

Maloney was almost blinded by the sun. His stomach churned, and he battled desperately to gather his jumbled wits. He put his hand above his goggles to try and see the approaching enemy aircraft. He heard and saw Adams' front Vickers machine gun spit fire and then the tracer and sparks from the bullet strikes. They had hit an oncoming whirling blur.

Suddenly two more Fokker DR1 triplanes whizzed down and past them on the port side. The closest of the triplanes was trailing a thin stream of smoke. The other veered sideways and down, displaying its undercarriage. It peeled away and chased a Sopwith Camel among the dispersing British planes. The entire squadron took evasive action. The scattered clatter of machine-gun fire came from all directions as several dogfights ensued.

'One of the Huns trailed smoke. I think you hit it, sir!' yelled Maloney into his voice pipe, turning the Scarff mount with the Lewis gun to port. He pulled back the bolt and locked it into position. His heart thumped wildly as the fighting instinct kicked in. No time for panic, this was a do or die contest. He pressed the lever under the Scarff ring mount and raised the hoop with the Lewis gun firmly attached. He had worked on the mounts many times and knew their functions well. He continued to swivel the gun on the Scarff ring mount around, looking for a passing enemy aircraft – knowing the angle of fire to be in front of the plane's flight path to compensate for distance and speed of flight when the bullets might reach the speeding target. Perhaps easier said than done. This was where the quick learning curve crept in. Hopefully, creeping in quick enough.

'I thought I saw sparks, old chap,' screamed Adams through the earphones in answer to

Maloney's first assessment of the enemy attack. 'Keep a look out for the Hun at the back. One will come in and try from your rear section. Be ready, Maloney. This show is just beginning.'

Some of the surrounding aircraft climbed with them, including Captain Polden in the other Bristol F2B. Maloney saw Elliott in his observer cockpit. The cadet swung his Scarff ring mount around as his Lewis gun searched for a target. The recruit had some skill and experience after a few days of flying missions. Elliott let loose with a four-round burst from his flank as a Fokker DR1 whooshed down past Captain Polden's Biff.

'Almost,' muttered Maloney, as Elliott turned around and stared directly at him. The cadet wore a big gratifying grin and gave Maloney a quick thumbs up. For a moment, Maloney thought the other aircraft observer had heard his muttering. Perhaps it was some sixth sense, and Elliott knew he was being watched. Maloney smiled back and returned the thumbs up gesture as the two Bristol F2Bs veered away from each other in search of an enemy to engage in combat.

Below, Vickers machine guns clattered away with regulation three and four-round bursts and so too were enemy Spandau machine guns. Maloney looked down; he saw the unfolding dogfight – a sequence of aerial contests. There was an explosion to the front of one Sopwith Camel as the triumphant German DR1 shot past. Another Sopwith Camel dropping behind the enemy triplane spat sporadic bursts of machine-gun fire. A sporadic tracer guiding the pilot's search for a revenge kill.

The stricken Sopwith Camel plunged into a burning dive, leaving a thick trail of smoke. Maloney gritted his teeth and searched the surrounding sky for any enemy planes that might dare to attack from the rear. Instantly his sight landed upon the approaching speck climbing in pursuit of their tail fin's new upward trajectory. 'One Hun incoming up on our tail, sir. My three o'clock! Arcing around to come from behind. Gradually getting central…'

'Tell me when it hits around two hundred yards. Ah, I have the little sod's prop on the mirror – very good, Maloney. It'll open up at around one hundred, I'm veering to port about…now!'

Maloney's heart jumped. Everything happened so fast. He almost lost concentration when he saw the starboard outboard-trailing wing's upper and lower ailerons dropping. The entire aircraft rolled rudely to port. He gulped and grabbed the cockpit rim, despite knowing his harness was secure. Understanding that the port ailerons would be lifting. Quickly, he got a grip of himself and lunged for the Lewis gun, turning the Scarff ring and gun elevation accordingly and skilfully adjusting for the aircraft's port roll – a split-second reflex action. The Lewis gun barrel was correctly ahead of the oncoming enemy triplane that was whizzing along, passing by their tail fin. Maloney squeezed the trigger. He caught sight of the blur – a rapidly moving mass as it shot past. The four-round burst of pa, pa, pa, pa! One tracer round among the projectiles and the arcing turn hit something within that wicked distorted mass.

No time to ponder. Swing of the Scarff ring. The passing and receding Fokker DR1 fin clear. Another four-round burst at the diminishing white tail fin. Somehow, Maloney still managed to follow the sudden upsurge of the enemy aircraft. Its flight path went straight up. He let loose with another four rounds as he felt their own aircraft lift. He saw two strikes on the exposed enemy fuselage fairing as another tracer round showed the rough course of his shooting.

Adams continued to climb and manoeuvre the Biff for Maloney's Scarff and Lewis to follow. The fledgling observer was able to let off another three-round burst to the front of the DR1's flight path just prior to it passing the course target. Again, another strike hit the enemy plane's upper starboard front wing tip as it turned while climbing. If it had been to the rear of the trailing wing, he might have smashed the aileron. No such luck. A few hits but Maloney assumed a few canvas rips at best.

The Fokker DR1 managed to climb some more before pitching off to fight elsewhere.

Adams' excited voice came through Maloney's earmuffs. 'That should give the cocky blighter something to think about. You got a few strikes in there, Maloney. You reacted well. Our Biff easily evaded the fixed enemy gun-sights.'

Maloney called back nervously, searching for anything new that might attack them. 'The tracer round bent as two visible strikes hit that light and dark green-flecked canvas fuselage, sir.'

'I saw it as I turned,' Adams called through the Gosport system. 'One bullet hole in the patterned section while the second strike put a hole in the square white background around the black Teutonic cross. A mere two punctures that wouldn't hinder the enemy aircraft as it shot past, but I bet that blooming Hun got the wind up good and proper. So, dashed well done, Maloney.'

'Two hits on the back canvas fuselage as well, sir. When it was climbing. Not enough to stop the Hun coming for a second helping,' Maloney called through his pipe, his adrenalin pulsating through his veins as his heart thumped excitedly. Fear being overwhelmed by the surrounding battle and the sharpness of much-needed wits.

'Again, well done, Maloney. It'll certainly give that fellow something to think about,' replied Lieutenant Adams as he took the Bristol F2B into another arcing port dive.

The excited pilot made for a dropping attack alongside a lower rolling and elaborately blue-coloured Fokker DR1 triplane. Its front engine cowling remained crimson red as were its wing struts, giving it a contrast against the main blue. The German pilot had just broken off an engagement against an evading Sopwith Camel. The screaming engine of Adams' diving Biff caught the small window of opportunity. An offering for a mere split-second burst. Adams timed the shots well. The five-round burst and the line of a tracer projectile showed the aim was good. Two strike punctures along the fuselage fairing and a third hit causing the exposed pilot to jerk spasmodically to the impact of the speeding projectile smashing down through the leather cap and the top of the wretched man's skull. Death would have been instant.

Maloney winced at the explosion of gore and thought his heart would leap from his mouth. He flinched and raised his arms as he expected their speeding downward assault would collide with the blue enemy aircraft. They swooped down, narrowly missing the white fin with its black Teutonic cross. He realised that the blue DR1 had remained functional, but the pilot must surely be dead. The entire aircraft just continued along a speeding preset course.

'That Hun took three close-quarter shots, sir,' Maloney yelled. 'Two holes moving along the fuselage fairing towards the pilot. I think he was killed by the third shot.'

'Yes, Maloney. I thought I caught sight of that third strike hitting the poor fellow. But better him than one of our own, old chap.'

The entire scene had been swift with wicked split-second clarity. Their Bristol F2B rolled away from the lame and retreating Fokker DR1. Adams steered the aircraft around; Maloney was able to quickly turn the Scarff ring mount and search the sky for any more incoming. All around, the dogfights continued. DR1s chasing Sopwith Camels or vice versa. Planes trailing smoke, some falling in flames.

Fleeting actions were locked in dreamlike split-second moments. Maloney marvelled at the visual information he could retain in such an instant. The image and the spasmodic jerk of the stricken enemy pilot also dumbfounded him.

As their two-seater Bristol F2B arced about, Maloney watched morbidly as the retreating blue Fokker DR1 began to slowly roll to port. Then all the way around until it was completely upside down – the distant slumped form of the dead pilot was motion-less and held inside the cockpit by his harness. Then the triplane proceeded from this upside-down position into a steep, diving head-on fall. Maloney tried not to take any notice. He looked up again at the surrounding dogfights, searching for other enemy planes that might attack. Alas, he kept stealing fleeting glances down at the serene upside-down nose-dive towards the earth at about seventy degrees. No smoke came from the healthy Fokker DR1 engine. Maloney looked up again and saw further machine-gun fire scattering over the duelling aircraft and then back down. Just one unnoticed, lonely descent to mother earth's lush multi-green-coloured meadows and the distant propeller sounding like a distressed buzzing fly leaving a room. The little mozzie departed from the fray and fell towards the inviting patchwork quilt of fields.

'The little meadows will look a lot bigger when you get closer,' Maloney whispered sympathetically and crossed himself in respect for the pilot inside the plummeting enemy triplane.

Back to the matter at hand. All around, the clatter of machine-gun fire, biplanes and enemy triplanes whizzed by – here, there and everywhere. The sky was alive with aircraft engines and rat-tling pa, pa, pa – ta, ta, ta. Explosions as engines ignited – others stalling and spluttering amid bullet punctures. Relentless wicked bursts of projectile fire everywhere. Spiralling trails of black smoke twisting and turning downwards towards a violent end.

'Keep an eye out for further incoming Huns, Maloney – there's a good chap!' called Adams through the trusted voice hose.

'Yes, sir,' replied Maloney, jumping to the task, and checking the Lewis gun and the air-cooling vents. All seemed in order. 'You got that one back there, sir. It's definitely on its way down. I saw the pilot dead inside the cockpit.'

Adams agreed. 'Did you see the pilot jolt by the bullet's impact? One minute a blood rush and a call of victory and then the gradual shame. But we may have to do this again. So, shame can wait until we're back and having a drink. A blooming good one.'

'Yes, sir,' Maloney replied, gripping the voice hose and then letting it drop.

'Let's keep our eyes peeled. This is not over yet,' Adams replied.

'Another one dropping down from the rear, sir! Eleven o'clock!' Maloney yelled.

Lieutenant Adams instantly reacted, pulling the ring-topped stick back and taking the Bristol F2B up another steep climb. For a few seconds, he exposed the colourful yellow and green-flecked fuselage fairing and the red cowling to Maloney's Lewis gun. A quick turn of the Scarff mount and a slight raise of the hoop with the gun-sights before the enemy's diving flight path.

To Maloney, the whole sequence was once again surreal. Almost in slow motion as he pulled the Lewis gun's trigger. He was aiming just ahead of the diving top section, taking advantage and letting loose with a six-round burst. The right bolt moved back and forth along the side as each used shell cap was flung from the weapon's side. He saw the tracer round bend towards the Fokker DR1 and one bullet strike hitting the top of the wing's central section and another hitting the red engine cowling just before the propeller. His mechanical mind kicked in. Even without knowledge of the Fokker engine, he had some idea of its make-up. Surely the bullet puncture had smashed through the sheeting and into one of the cylinders of the rotary engine? If it miraculously missed any of the cylinders, then perhaps it smashed through the engine bay back-plate and other workings? Hopefully smashing tappets and causing proper damage as the Fokker DR1 soared downwards and past their climbing Bristol F2B. He gulped with excitement. That had to be a crippling strike. Definitely a top form of engine damage. Maloney hollered into the voice pipe, 'Now I'll be betting you that horrid bright yellow, green and red colour does wonders for the migraine sufferer.' His humour was masking the mixture of fear and excitement. A potent rush of his mixed adrenalin.

'I'll second that one, Maloney.' Lieutenant Adams laughed. What else could they do? They were fighting for their lives in a vicious dogfight.

Maloney managed a brief look down before Adams rolled the Bristol F2B onto another flight path. 'You hit it twice,' called Adams. 'Dashed well done, Maloney. One of the strikes hit the engine cowling.'

Maloney was looking down at the Fokker DR1's yellow and green-flecked fuselage as the plane levelled out and headed east. 'I know, sir. I can see a thin stream of smoke coming out. Do you reckon that might be a kill? It seems to be making for a retreating home run.'

'I think it's possible you may have one kill. But I bet even that's unconfirmed. If the one you hit goes down, it will also be unconfirmed. No team points for them, I'm afraid, even if they do crash. Back to the gun-sights, old chap. This isn't over yet. The Hun will want a few of us for dinner. Let's try and make it costly,' yelled Adams.

'Oh, for the love of God!' hissed Maloney in horrific shock. Both he and Adams gulped as Captain Polden's Bristol F2B rolled down and around past them in the opposite direction, each man having time to drink in the dreadful sight. Captain

Polden struggled with the controls while thick black smoke escaped from the hidden side of his grey engine cowling. Maloney's mouth dropped open as he watched in horror. He reasoned that Captain Polden's aircraft had bullet strikes near the exhaust manifold. These punctures would have smashed into the Wolseley Viper's one hundred and eighty h.p. engine. An engine now shattered and burning with leaking oil, fire and smoke devouring the front of the aircraft. An angry propeller still whirring. Laboured parts still trying to function.

'I think he's trying to turn off a fuel feed,' called Maloney.

'No doubt the Jones valve, Maloney. It's usually that one first.' Adams scoured the blue sky. Captain Polden was already lost as he pathetically wrestled with his controls. There was nothing anyone could do for him.

'I never thought to see Captain Polden go down,' Maloney whispered to himself. Then he hissed and recoiled in disgust. His vision ran along Polden's smoking craft as they circled the dreadful scene. There was Elliott. The now dead cadet observer. He was lying slumped back in the rear of his cockpit. His head facing up to the sky in gaping, open-mouthed surprise. His flying goggles were gone. An empty socket remained. The surrounding flesh was caked in blood around the great cavity where his right eye once was. The back of his leather flying hat was a mass of ripped leather and bloodied gore. Only the harnesses held the dead man in place. His blood cascading down and along the green canvas where more bullet holes were visible along the upper fuselage fairing. Once again, the fleeting image offered much in such a brief moment.

Then an arcing yellow-painted Fokker DR1 fell in behind Polden's smoking Bristol F2B. Still with the striking red contrast of the propeller casing against the yellow fuselage. No doubt the fighter ace who had already caused the damage. A predator making sure of his kill. It fell behind Polden's thick trail of black smoke, following the aircraft's gently descending wake, gradually flying closer before letting loose with a further burst from its twin Spandau guns. There was nothing Adams or Maloney could do as their aircraft turned about in the vicious extravaganza of aerial duelling. Maloney was able to catch a glimpse of the final moments of Captain Polden's burning aircraft as they circled above. There followed further bullet strikes and sparks as Maloney noticed one of the wing struts on Polden's machine snap. A further hit along the already smoking engine casing. The ticking tappets spluttered and stalled as a small fiery explosion erupted from the hood casing. Captain Polden slumped forward onto the wooden control panel. The Bristol F2B then plunged into a steep screaming dive. A mass of wicked flames spewed from the engine cowling, streaming back and becoming a furious cloak of fire, overlapping the dead pilot and observer. Flames that engulfed all, cooking them inside the plummeting aircraft. A burning furnace leaving a trail of thick black smoke while plunging down. Plummeting towards the placid meadows below.

'Maloney, keep your eyes peeled. Have that Lewis at the ready, there's a good chap. That fancy Hun might like us for a double kill.'

Once again, Adams took the Bristol F2B into a flanking roll and veered around the aerial battle scene. On all quarters, the vicious dogfight was in full flow. A light blue Fokker DR1 with the usual red propeller casing trailed smoke while a Sopwith gave chase, firing away on its twin Vickers machine guns. And then in the opposite direction came another burning plane. This time a smoking British fighter chased by a German triplane with square multi-coloured tiles of dark green, light green, grey and black. Again, with red propeller-surround cowling.

'Another coming in at the fin,' yelled Maloney as a new Fokker DR1 dived down towards them. 'My word! This one has a black fuselage with red prop casing.'

Adams lifted the plane instantly while rolling to port. Maloney quickly adjusted by swivelling the

Scarff ring mount. The strong sense of emergency had him pointing the Lewis gun to meet the diving attack. He managed to let off a quick four-round burst. He heard the enemy's twin Spandau guns' rapid and synchronised return fire. Neither duellists struck their target in the quick set-to. The enemy plane plunged past and beneath them while Maloney quickly compensated his position, swiftly swinging the Scarff ring from port to starboard and pointing down at the light blue fuselage fairing. A second burst of three rounds, but the Fokker DR1 had dropped low very quickly. He was about to let off another burst but thought better of it as Lieutenant Adams levelled their aircraft. The enemy plane was already speeding away then coming in at a distance.

'I think it's circling, sir,' said Maloney.

Neither he nor Lieutenant Adams saw the incoming drop attack from the sun. The short burst of synchronised Spandau fire opened up before Adams could give the word. A bullet hit the middle of the upper central wing and ripped down through the canvas to strike Lieutenant Adams' wicker wood backrest. He jumped and twisted with a look of wincing pain. Simultaneously, two more bullet strikes punctured the fuselage fairing along the rear, each strike moving away from Maloney's rear cockpit. The young observer winced and gritted his teeth. He wondered how on earth he had been missed by those following two bullets. The fleeting glimpse of the multi-green streaks along the Fokker DR1's upper tri-wings and fuselage and the red wing struts, wheels, undercarriage frame and propeller casing shot past at close quarters as it continued to nosedive. Then the patterned enemy plane veered away at a lower altitude. Maloney gasped and tried to calm himself. The second triplane began to circle widely and gently climb. No doubt for a second attack that would come behind the tail fin. Maloney quickly gathered his wits and lunged forward. He pulled the Lewis gun bolt back. This time he would be waiting as he brought the Scarff mounting about to point his Lewis and be ready for the next attack. Where was the yellow DR1 that had circled them?

Before he could make ready, the Bristol F2B suddenly and unexpectedly plunged into a steep dive. The engine raced in protest. Was the dive intentional? Or was Lieutenant Adams hit? Maloney was hoping it was just the lieutenant's chair. He felt his harness go taut as he lunged towards the Lewis gun handles. Then he fell backwards into his cockpit and upon the backrest of his seat – then bone-shaking turbulence as the Bristol F2B began its structural protest. Maloney's disorientated senses quickly shredded away to the terrifying realisation that their plane was going down, falling headlong into a dive. Desperately, he struggled against the harness straps and turned and looked forward in the direction of the head-on descent. The super rush of the elements. The rising scream of the engine, the whirr of the propeller beyond the light grey engine cowling. Below, the colourful uneven rectangles and squares growing larger by the second. This was it, they were going down. Was Lieutenant Adams dead? He was sprawled forward, lying upon the lever stick, pressing it against the wood-clad control panel. Blood was running down the leather clothing of his left shoulder. Maloney tried to struggle forward and stretch across into Adams' cockpit. He wanted to grab the stick's circular lever and pull it back, but Adams was harnessed in the seat with his slumped form in the way. Even if Maloney could move the dead weight, how would he know what to do? Could he control the diving plane? The engine continued to scream in protest, racing to a crescendo – the fields and trees continued to grow larger as they came up towards him at the speed of his life.

'Oh my God!' muttered Maloney, stretching out of his observer's cockpit across to the pilot's. With his outstretched arm he tried to move aside Adams' immobile body to grab the circular spoon handle of the lever stick as the wind rushed past him. The engine screamed its horrifying decent. The patchwork of green grew ominously large. The whole aircraft, a plummeting and violently shaking structure. How feeble the canvas-wrapped frame was – how cheap life was. How petrifying it all was. He opened his mouth and screamed with fear and outright rage, 'No, no, no!'

A VISIT FROM THE GRIM REAPER

'I wonder what our Maloney is doing right now,' muttered Cooper as he stared around the empty hangar tent.

'Well, I would like to say he's enjoying himself, but that's not very likely knowing our Maloney,' replied Norris.

'Is there not one small part of him that wonders what it's like to go up in a kite he's been looking after and maintaining for so long?' Tibbit was still hoping there might be something more positive about the opportunity to go flying.

'No!' Norris and Cooper replied.

Tibbit pursed his lips and blew out a steady stream of air. 'Well it's nice to see you blokes saying what you mean.'

'Tibby,' Norris began. 'We have said it once. Please believe us—'

'For the love of God, believe us,' Cooper cut in.

Norris acknowledged his friend's back-up support, then looked back at Tibbit and continued, 'There is nothing romantic about going up in this air campaign. There's nothing gallant about any part of this entire blooming war. It is something that has to be done, I admit. But the air war is one area where a very high percentage of these airmen will not stay the distance. Most of them are officers and the stop-at-homes, here on the airfield, are lower ranks. The one area where we stand a better chance of survival than the officers. The casualty rate is very excessive among the flying men. Just learn to repair the kites and stay away from learning anything that you don't need to know. Show no aptitude or enthusiasm for anything other than repair work.'

'I know what you're saying, and I agree.' Tibbit looked stressed. 'But if you are put in one of those observer cockpits and find yourself up there through no fault of your own, surely you must do your best in order to try and survive.'

'Well, that goes without saying,' Cooper added. 'But part of your situation is not to be seconded by not being too enthusiastic to learn things. I can't emphasise this enough. There will be no fault of your own because you'll not find yourself in such a cockpit. That's the aim, Tibby. We are repeating ourselves, but you should live and breathe this.'

'Fine. I understand. At the risk of us going around and around in circles, is there anything else we can talk about? There must be something we can all find more appealing.' Tibbit beamed hopefully.

Norris grinned. 'At least the tea is hot, and we have some of the birthday boy's cake left. How about that? We could each take a slice for this afternoon tea.'

Cooper sighed and looked back to Tibbit, then nodded towards Norris. 'There is taking a liberty, and then there's Norris. Liberty taking is not the word for this bloke.'

Tibbit nodded. 'Don't you think we should wait for Dermot to return?'

To Tibbit's surprise, it was Cooper who erupted with a deep belly laugh, saying, 'The lad has taken me seriously.'

'I thought you wanted to...' Tibbit lingered while the two old mechanics were filled with further mirth.

'He's so easy to rankle,' Norris said, laughing.

'I do like a raw recruit with all those fine principles and things. There's a clean naivety about them,' continued Cooper.

'I can remember when our Maloney was like that.' Norris chuckled, cutting a slice of Maloney's birthday carrot cake.

'Well, Tibby. If you don't want your bit of Maloney's birthday cake, Norris and I'll shall help you out,' added Cooper craftily.

'Oh no. I didn't mean it like that,' replied Tibbit. He was rather fond of carrot cake.

Cooper and Norris sniggered at the young recruit's reply. 'We're not making fun of you, Tibby me old fruit. We're just enjoying you,' said Norris, trying to suppress further giggles.

Tibbit quickly calmed down and saw the humour in it all. 'You know, you two blokes take the biscuit when it comes to a little twirl. Maybe one day something will come along and slap you back with a bigger leg-pull. One that will scare the pants off you before you realise everything is fine.'

'Well, as long as everything turns out fine, who can complain in the end?' said Cooper, chuckling as he poured the hot tea from the kettle.

Norris frowned as he looked through the tent hangar's opening and across the turf. 'He's doing the rounds early. He must have certain information about someone and he's making for our hangar.'

'Bloody hell. I don't like the look of this,' said Cooper as he watched Lieutenant Carruthers walk purposefully towards their tent.

'It's just Lieutenant Carruthers,' said Tibbit.

Norris sighed fearfully. 'The bloody Grim Reaper is his nickname, Tibby, and he's coming here to see us. The aircrew are not here, and he only sees us when there's bad news concerning the aircrew.'

Cooper shuddered. 'Something has happened, and they have information via other airfield aircraft returns. Pilots that have seen aircraft go down. Ours aren't back yet. Other pilots at another airfield probably are. And they have bad news. Then the top brass get on the blower to Major Laws and then off goes the Grim Reaper with his swag bag of bad news.'

Slowly and with trepidation, the three aircraft mechanics moved to the big tent's opening. Each noted the regretful sigh on Lieutenant Carruthers' face. It was very grim indeed. He stopped before them and looked down, holding his clipboard. He always walked about with a clipboard.

'I'm so very sorry, men, but I have some dreadful news. Evidently, there has been a huge dogfight over the mission area. A real old scrap. We have reports of several Bristol F2Bs going down. We know one is Captain Polden and Cadet Observer Elliott. Both chaps have bought it, I'm afraid.'

All three men were deeply shocked and saddened by the news. Captain Polden was very well liked, and they were growing very fond of Elliott.

'Blimey, sir,' Cooper said. 'Elliott wasn't here long. I thought Captain Polden was one who might make it.'

'I know what you mean, Cooper.' Carruthers was genuinely sorry.

'Is there any news of Lieutenant Adams and Acting Observer Maloney, sir?' Tibbit asked.

Carruthers gritted his teeth and sighed again. It was obvious he was uncomfortable about saying the next part of the news he had. Norris gulped as Cooper dropped his head in sorrow. Tibbit's mouth opened as though he were about to yell. He had only met Maloney this morning, surely the poor fellow couldn't be dead already.

'We know it went into a dive after being hit by an attack. No one saw the plane crash, but it went into a dive. There was no smoke, and no one saw it hit the ground.' Carruthers sighed. It was obvious that he didn't have much hope.

Norris, Cooper and Tibbit all dropped their heads. This was dreadful. Both planes on one flight. Surely not?

NOT YET OLD CHAP

Suddenly, Lieutenant Adams lurched in his damaged wicker chair backrest and robustly pulled the cloth-bound ringed lever with him. Maloney fell back into his observer's cockpit, shocked and dazed. His hands gripping the rear cockpit rim for dear life. His face wore a look of terror. He screamed through the voice hose, 'Blooming hell, sir – sure I thought you were dead there, so I did.'

'Not yet, old chap.' Adams groaned and pulled the lever for all it was worth.

The descending plane screamed its whirling protest while sluggishly levelling out at around a thousand feet altitude, eventually flying straight over fields and trees in enemy territory before making way for a steep climb. Suddenly, flak exploded about them and projectile fire from ground-based rifles could be heard. The scattered crackles warned of bullets whizzing about them.

Maloney gasped with relief and called, 'Where the Devil is all this flak coming from? We're not over the front lines.'

'The enemy has anti-aircraft guns out here, Maloney. Look over there. Mounted on trucks. We have them too.'

'God love us.' Maloney looked about in shock as the grey smoke of the shells continued to explode about their ascending aircraft. Little puffs of smouldering tendrils fanned out and spread shrapnel. Fortunately, nothing was close to them and each moment they climbed, the better their situation became against ground forces.

'I think we can do this, Maloney,' Adams' voice hissed in the Gosport system.

'I know I've already said it, sir. But, my God – I thought you were dead, so I did. I thought the pair of us were goners, that's for sure.'

'And as I've already said,' Adams sniggered, 'not yet, old chap.

Let's get this kite back up.'

'You're bleeding from the back, sir! I can see it on the leather. Your left shoulder. But I'm glad you can still handle this kite,' said Maloney with relief and gratitude. 'I'm not sure if I thank you, sir, or the Almighty.'

'I've stopped something. It's in my shoulder, old boy,' mumbled Adams, ignoring the God part of Maloney's words while taking the Bristol F2B up and away from the flak and bullets. 'I think it's the ricochet from the chair's backrest. I had you install that curved metal strip around the wicker back. I think the bullet hit that.'

'I definitely saw the bullet strike the seat, sir,' Maloney replied, looking over the fin at the retreating ground which seemed to be getting pleasingly smaller and further away from the flak explosions. 'Long live this climb.'

'My left arm is certainly causing some pain, but let's try and get this kite out of this. We're fleeing from ground fire to return to the blooming hell of dogfighting. We need the height and will be better off taking our chances up here than at low altitude.'

'I'm completely with you on that one, sir. I'm finding this horrid height much more appealing now.' Maloney checked his work as he pulled back the bolt of the Lewis gun. There were still plenty of shells and other drum magazines within easy reach. 'Back to the fray, sir.'

The sporadic shots had stopped, plus the flak was too low and diminishing. Maloney looked about; he could see that the dogfighting had dispersed over a wider expanse.

'The duels are happening a long way off,' Adams muttered as he brought the Bristol F2B into a levelling position while pilot and observer instinctively searched the skies.

'I'm keeping my eyes peeled, sir. Especially that sun. The Hun fighter pilots do seem to like that glaring cover when attacking.' Maloney gulped, trying to search the glare with the aid of his goggle shades. As he drew his attention away from the sun, his lowered vision caught sight of the two Fokker DR1s arcing around upon their tail from a distance.

'Two of them coming about from the rear on my right side, sir,' Maloney called out, grabbing the grips of the Lewis gun and getting ready.

'I've got them in the rear mirror, old chap,' Adams gasped through his pain barrier. Blood oozed down the leather material on his left arm. This was bad. He knew it was on the inside too. He could feel the sticky gore running along his flesh. A dull but continuous throbbing had replaced the sharp pain of the original hit before he had blacked out momentarily and awoken to the ground rushing towards him.

'They're both coming in, sir. Probably closing for the hundred yards burst,' yelled Maloney.

'Hold tight, Maloney, and let me know when they're between three and two hundred and fifty yards. If I can still gauge them in the rear-view mirrors I'll act, but feel free to say when you judge the distance and then hold on dashed tightly.'

Maloney turned back and looked at his pilot, alarmed by the tone. He knew the lieutenant would do something most outrageous against the two rapidly approaching enemy aircraft, both of which had fallen in line. The blue backdrop reflected their whirring props and thin tri-wings. One behind the other for a double burst and flanking veer cut-off to move away and evade. If necessary, circle and attack again.

As the judged three hundred yards were reached, Maloney screamed into the voice hose, 'Three hundred and closing, sir.' He briefly remembered the tail elevators lifting.

At the same time Lieutenant Adams hissed, 'Hold tight, old chap.' He pulled the ring-topped stick towards him and pressed himself against the seat's shredded backrest, and the Bristol F2B abruptly pitched upwards. While climbing high the Falcon engine screamed and the plane arced backwards and over. Both the pilot and observer were now upside down. Once again, Maloney was completely disoriented, feeling as though the contents of his stomach might fall through his gullet and out into the slipstream. They were doing the looping the loop manoeuvre.

'God – love us,' Maloney muttered to himself, wanting to squeeze his eyes shut.

Their heads were raised upwards in the plane. Their upside-down necks and heads looking down. Gulping Adam's apples wobbling nervously as each man saw the commotion below. Both Fokker DR1 triplanes passed beneath the looping upside-down Bristol F2B. The horrid green-flecked Fokker DR1 was one of them. The other was grey with red cowling by the propeller.

The Bristol F2B began to arc right over and turn downwards to straighten up snuggly behind the two enemy planes' tail fins. Maloney had heard of looping the loop but never expected to experience it. He turned and looked over Lieutenant Adams' shoulder and sighed in relief. There was a slight smile of satisfaction at the sight of the light and dark green-streaked plane before the pilot's Vickers machine gun. The very triplane that had dived and wounded Lieutenant Adams in the last attack. The other grey one was a little ahead. Its starboard aileron suddenly dropped while its port aileron raised. The whole grey mass rolled port side and away from the pursuing Bristol F2B. Maybe to come about while Adams went for the remaining Fokker DR1. As the rolling grey triplane dropped and fell away to port, Maloney turned the Scarff and the Lewis towards the falling away aircraft. He tried to judge the forward trajectory a little ahead of the enemy aircraft making its way from them, even pulling and locking the bolt in readiness to let loose a burst. Alas, no. The speeding dive was too quick and too far to waste a short burst of bullets. Wait for a surer target.

'They all seem to like that same touch of red, sir.' Maloney frowned as the green-flecked enemy aircraft tried to break away, rolling in the opposite starboard direction. Maloney's jumbled wits had been settling. Coming out of the looping the loop confusion. Then he was off into a fresh bout of mystification as he had a split second to notice their aircraft's starboard aileron lift, knowing the port-side aileron would drop.

Lieutenant Adams rolled starboard and dropped, chasing after the triplane that arced down, desperate to escape from their trick manoeuvre. They had a score to settle with this green-flecked aircraft. Maloney watched in amazement as his injured pilot skilfully anticipated the trajectory of the enemy aircraft's starboard yaw. The close turning enemy crossed their own rolling line of flight. For a moment, the Fokker DR1 became a large target. Within that split-second time frame, Lieutenant Adams fired his Vickers machine gun.

Both aircrew of the Bristol F2B knew what would happen before the synchronised machine gun's bullets were unleashed. The four-round burst of pa, pa, pa, pa delivered the collective cluster of projectiles with wicked satisfaction.

Maloney winced and gritted his teeth. His wicked delight was apparent as strikes punctured the enemy's engine cowling by one of the Spandau guns, a second ripping into the outboard aileron of the top wing, plus another strike into the fuselage just behind the pilot's seat. Maloney knew the engine hit would be potentially destructive and that the shell hitting the upper wing section might cause cables, bell cranks or pulley systems to malfunction too. There had to be telling damage from such a hit. Though there was no time to notice the development of such damage. Adams' urgent voice needlessly screamed out as he rolled into a yaw while turning the Bristol F2B's flight path again.

'Stand by with the Lewis, old chap!'

The opportunity had already been spotted as Maloney jumped to his own reflex action. His rear-facing Lewis gun turned on the mount just in time. He realised instantly that the arcing enemy triplane would present him with a quick chance shot too. He managed a three-round burst and was uplifted by two noticeable hits shredding the close-quarter rear elevator and rudder's canvas as their flight path carried them down past the damaged and evading enemy aircraft.

'Hit the rear rudder and side tail elevator, sir. Now I think I might be getting the hang of this,' yelled Maloney as excitement coursed throughout his body.

Lieutenant Adams put the plane back into the turning climb, looking for the second triplane that might be circling for another rear attack. Neither of them could spot the second grey Fokker DR1. Maloney squinted up into the sun, but saw nothing.

Other planes were still duelling in the distance amid the blue as their Bristol F2B plane turned westwards, back towards the front line and home territory.

'Keep those eyes of yours peeled, Maloney.' Adams coughed. His painful discomfort was still obvious.

'I will do, sir,' Maloney replied, scouring the sky above and below from his observer's cockpit. Also noting the distant smoking trail of the injured Fokker DR1 aircraft they had attacked. It was flying eastwards away from its duel in the sky.

'Trust me, Maloney.' Adams gasped while wrestling with the stick's ringed grip and controls. 'The bigger aces usually tend to look from a higher altitude. People leaving the dogfight like us are now prime targets. The more experienced Hun will know that this type of aircraft with an observer is likely to have photographs. We're a prize target for the ace who likes a stray, and this lot are the Red Baron's Jagdgeschwader I squadron. All with their partial reds here and there against varied canvas colours or other silly patterns. This is what's often called the flying circus. The Baron von Richthofen will be somewhere unless he's already gone after a lone prize. Keep looking up and at that sun on regular occasions. Also, from below. I wouldn't put it past one sneaky Hun to come from below.'

'Do you really think the Red Baron was with this squadron then, sir?'

'Without any shadow of a doubt, Maloney. The Baron is a complete predator, and I repeat, we're the type of target he likes. A stray leaving the battle.'

'Perhaps he was among the other triplanes in the dogfight?' Maloney suggested.

Adams continued to battle the pain in his left arm and side. He wanted to talk to keep himself alert. 'Most of the other triplanes had those red-painted sections around the propeller casing and wheel struts. The flying circus planes have unique little oddities for each plane. At least it seems that way. The Baron von Richthofen usually keeps most of his plane red. Even the front casing section before the propeller. I also think the black Teutonic cross isn't in a square white frame either. It's straight on the red canvas as far as I can recall. However, I think the tail fin is white with the black Teutonic cross.'

'That shouldn't be too hard to spot, sir,' Maloney replied through the voice pipe.

Lieutenant Adams smiled as he battled with his trustworthy Biff. The plane had performed well so far.

THE SOMBRE HANGAR

Cooper lit a cigarette by the tea table. Lieutenant Carruthers had instructed them all to sit down and have a cup of tea and a smoke. The officer would be back if he heard any more news. The air mechanic tossed the packet before Norris, who gratefully accepted then offered the pack to Tibbit, who politely declined.

Tibbit was looking for any grain of hope and made a suggestion. 'They did say there was no smoke when Lieutenant Adams went into a dive after the attack. Perhaps it was an evasive action.'

Cooper nodded dumbfounded, drawing upon his cigarette. His eyes stared outside of the hangar onto the airfield, but they were vacant as though he were somewhere else.

Norris leaned back and blew out a thin stream of smoke before replying to Tibbit. 'Could be, Tibby. They did say no smoke and I agree that it could be an evasive action. But dropping low to evade the enemy is not the normal thing to do. Especially our Lieutenant Adams. He loves to climb with his treasured Falcon III engine. He thinks his Biff falls upwards.'

'Dropping increases the danger of ground attack coming from all directions,' added Cooper, still staring outside at the damp green grass and the various personnel going about their duties.

'I wish that Major Laws were out at another airfield when young Cadet Sullivan was taken ill. I doubt whether Captain Polden would have made Maloney go up as an acting observer. That's where some of the upper-crust snobbery comes in handy. Especially for us lads.'

Tibbit looked puzzled. 'So, does Major Laws spend most of his time moving from one airfield to another?'

'He does,' replied Cooper. 'In between staying at the top brass hotel. A sort of large house which is a few miles further back. I've delivered and picked up things there a few times. A rather nice-looking place – a chateau I think it's called. I suppose he gets his orders and briefings, or whatever it is that top brass people do from this place.'

Norris added, 'The major seems to turn up at an airfield and takes over for a few days then moves on after upsetting the normal flow of things. I don't think the other officers and pilots enjoy Major Laws and his visits. Not just our airfield, but others too.'

'So, the major upsets the flow of things for a few days, then moves off to another airfield to do the same thing all over again?' Tibbit said.

'I think our Captain Polden was usually glad to see the back of the major, but never said as much,' said Cooper as he took a swig of his tea and then drew on his cigarette.

'Well, Captain Polden won't be doing it this time,' replied Norris sadly. 'His kite was ours. We thought we'd have him all the time. A real survivor.'

'We've seen this before, Norris,' said Cooper angrily at the outcome of the recent mission.

'I know, but how many more of these blokes are we going to see fall? We liked Captain Polden. He was a blooming good bloke. So was young Elliott. What chance did that poor little sod have?' Norris took another swig of tea.

Cooper nodded. 'We all moan about officers, but would you want to be one of those young lieutenants flying these kites? We make fun of Carruthers but to be fair to the man, I can't blame him for wanting to keep his backside in that pen-pusher's chair.'

Tibbit stood up and paced about the table, holding his tin mug of tea. He sighed. 'I've only been here a few hours now, but the reality of all this is not what I expected. Things are much more...' He searched for the appropriate word.

'Intense?' Cooper suggested.

'Yes,' Tibbit agreed. 'That's it – intense. I never realised we would be going through such things like this. We're sitting here at such close quarters. Not on the mission, but still fearful.'

'Imagine what it must be like for the blokes up in the kites,' added Norris.

'I'm trying to figure it out by looking at you two. Everyone is chewing their nails down to their blooming elbows. I can understand it too. I've met four aircrew only a few hours ago, including Dermot Maloney. And now they're probably dead.'

'Sometimes we can go for weeks without a death. It's very rare, but it does happen. Today looks like a bad one,' Norris scoffed sadly then drew on his cigarette.

'Four men all from this hangar,' agreed Cooper.

Tibbit added, 'That officer you called the Grim Reaper went over to one of the other hangars where Burke and Hare are. I suppose those two have had a bit of bad news too.'

'Hold up, lads,' Norris called, lifting his head and frowning. 'The Grim Reaper's coming back.'

'Is this another confirmation for Lieutenant Adams and our Maloney?' hissed Cooper.

'I think he's wearing a positive look,' Tibbit said with hope.

As Lieutenant Carruthers entered the tent hangar, he held up a placating hand. 'I don't want you chaps to get too carried away, but we have had further news from another airfield where another Sopwith has returned. He is adamant that Lieutenant Adams pulled out of his downward dive and climbed up back into the fray and engaged two Hun aircraft. Did a loop the loop and fell in behind them. Scattered the pair and managed to shoot one up. Sent it packing and trailing smoke by all accounts.'

'How come our aircrew has not returned while these Sopwith Camel planes that saw the dogfight have?' Cooper was still very sceptical and worried.

Another Bristol F2B came along the grass runway as flight mechanics from another tent hangar ran out joyfully to meet their returned charge. Cooper looked to Norris as Tibbit realised that both men longed to do the same thing.

A siren suddenly sounded as a fire engine and ambulance motored across the turf towards the runway.

'Another incoming – trailing smoke,' shouted someone as people chased the fire engine and the ambulance.

'Whose kite is that?' Cooper asked with a look of hope.

All, including Lieutenant Carruthers, walked out of the hangar to see the commotion. As they followed the flow of men they broke into a jog, along with the rest of the personnel, chasing the fire engine and ambulance out onto the open airfield.

'It's probably one of the other hangars' kites,' grumbled Norris, hurrying along and watching other ground crew men scurrying from neighbouring tent hangars. All hoped for one of their own aircrews to be returning.

'We've lost one crew,' puffed Cooper. 'Please don't let it be both of our charges.'

THE DREADFUL SURPRISE

'Are you alright, Maloney?' shouted Lieutenant Adams through the Gosport system. The ice-cold breeze lapped about them, but the Falcon III engine's purr was still delightful. It sounded fine.

Maloney yelled back through his voice pipe, 'Yes, sir. I'm just coming down a bit too fast. Feels strange after that blazing set-to back there.' He was gazing at the blue, scrutinising the clouds above and the wisps of white vapour between them and the lined hedgerows and meadows of various shades of green below. The pockmarked earth of the front was still some way off. He hoped they were not over-confident about their sudden survival during the horrific sequence of dogfights.

'I thought so. That's why I asked,' Adams bellowed back into his voice funnel. He was still under a lot of pain and stress but battled with the plane to keep their homeward-bound course true. Even shouting through the Gosport system, above the wind-rush, had caused discomfort. Neither of the airmen were angry, though their continued shouting would have caused an onlooker to believe they were. The loud calling had to be in place to combat the elements and the roaring aircraft engine. The pilot continued to shout, 'Sometimes tense fighting and the sudden come-down is as difficult as the conflict. A very unsettling experience, old chap.'

Maloney admired Lieutenant Adams' resolve. The pilot was made of a better substance than he could have imagined as an air mechanic. He smiled to himself and scoffed back humorously, 'I'm beginning to realise the coming-down thing, sir. Once again, we're exposed to the icy elements. That's a relief to have a new sense to grapple with. The cold vanished without me noticing during that shoot-out. Now I find it a welcome intrusion.'

'I know exactly what you mean, Maloney. You did very well back there. Very well indeed. But now – thank God for the icy fresh air. It makes us grateful to still be alive.'

Maloney shook his head in disbelief as he called back into the Gosport hose system. 'I'm shifting through a feeling of sudden reprieve. And it's very eerie, sir. But I thank God for it. I think of those poor fellows who went down. None of them will know this anymore.'

'Best to put those thoughts to the back of your mind, Maloney. Keep a sharp eye out for the enemy. The lone wolf will always try to drop upon us from the sun. As I've said, that's one of von Richthofen's methods. He likes lone observer aircrafts like this.'

'I will, sir.'

'I'm presuming we got some good photos back there, Maloney?'

'I think we got some splendid shots, sir.' Maloney peered up through his squinting eyes. Was that something flickering in the sun? No, nothing.

He gulped in more cold air. Uplifted by the fresh sensation, their venerable Bristol F2B serenely travelled westward, bound for home. The memory of enemy clatter of machine-gun fire was slowly fading. The whipping breeze was now invigorating.

Let's hope it's over now, Maloney thought. Again, he smiled gratifyingly to himself. His nostrils flared as he took in the cold air amid the rumbling engine coupled with the rotating propeller and the continuous elevating rush of the airstream. He looked along the fuselage fairing.

'Is everything in order back there, Maloney?'

'It is, sir. I'm looking at the two punctures in the fuselage fairing. Those two little bullet holes that just missed me.'

'I think the first one that hit my chair was a ricochet strike,' said Lieutenant Adams. 'My back and the bloodied rip in my left shoulder is causing some pain, but I don't think the bullet's in my flesh. I think it skimmed the shoulder and the coat. It was bewildering for a while.'

'Aye, that it was, sir. It certainly had me worried, that's for sure,' Maloney said casually.

Adams looked in his side mirror and joked about it. 'It certainly put me on my toes when I came to. All those lush fields coming to meet us with a nice kiss goodbye.'

'I thought it was very impressive, sir. That last-minute pull turned the plane from deep dive to a sudden upward climbing pitch amid that torrid ground fire of exploding flak and whizzing bullets. How on earth we came out of that, I'll never know.'

Once again, Maloney looked back along the fuselage fairing. He shuddered at the prospect of bullets striking him or the engine casing. One of the puncture holes was twelve inches from his observer cockpit. How close that was – one tiny projectile in the right place and that could have been it. He looked out at the wings and the canvas covering, understanding all the various cables and bell cranks that worked the ailerons and elevators. Knowing how easily one small malfunction could come about when projectiles smashed through such fragile mechanisms. He returned his scrutiny to the bullet strikes on the fuselage fairing. All the cables must have remained intact as the bullets shot through the top of the canvas and probably ripped out beneath. He was fortunate that the trajectory passed harmlessly through and missed the delicate inner cable workings. Other aircraft had not been so lucky. Would he ever be free of those horrifying sights? Dreadful moments when burning aircraft plunged to earth – British and enemy fighters alike.

What a horrid way to go, he thought to himself, shuddering. At any moment, it could have been him and Lieutenant Adams among those wretched souls falling through the sky in a burning wreck.

'It almost happened,' he whispered as his face twisted in disgust, noting the flimsy yet taut fabric wrapped around the Bristol F2B fuselage frame. The material covering did nothing to protect aircrew and petrol tanks. How vulgar and pointless the human waste was for all airmen on both sides of the conflict.

All the resulting death and destruction for a few photos. Maloney shook his head at the thought. Somehow their aircraft had survived the fearsome gun-blazing duels with all its twisting and turning during the aerial combat. That was down to Lieutenant Adams' skill. Maloney had to remind himself of that. His entire perspective of the lieutenant had changed for the better. He was a sound fellow.

'Look about the sky,' he scolded to himself. 'Be positive. No more dwelling on what happened.'

The young supplementary observer willed himself to gaze at the blue sky amid the persistent propeller's whirl, checking the odd fluffy cloud for a dark speck of movement. Nothing could be discerned. There he and Adams were, seemingly alone in the sky. Where were the others? Everyone else had scattered. Or was it just Lieutenant Adams that had separated from the main body? Maloney took another deep breath of cold refreshing air and decided to change the Lewis gun drum magazine. There could only be a maximum of ten rounds left. He wanted a full mag for anything that might drop on them. A full drum would always be better and all ninety-seven rounds at his disposal were the best he could have. It was no good running out of bullets and having to change in the middle of an attack. It would give the enemy time to get close and fire a concentrated burst.

Once again, Maloney gulped and wished his heart would stop racing. The cold air was helping but he could still see his hands shaking as he slid the centre of the drum magazine over the central hub.

After his first air combat, Maloney realised he couldn't have truly understood dread despite being told of such things. Now he had experienced the terrifying event, witnessed things for real. Before, he could never have fully appreciated how desperate a battle in the sky really was. But now he had become such an individual filled with experience. One that would rather have remained ignorant of such horrors.

The reluctant observer finally had his Lewis machine gun at the ready with a full complement of .303 bullets. It was a consolation that helped his mind settle. Memories of falling fire-ridden aircraft and horrid death slowly receded. Now, he wanted something else to concentrate on. Anything that could distract him further from the dreadful killing spree and that volume of sky where multiple dogfights had occurred. Little things here and there. Loading the Lewis gun while he continued to breathe the ice-cold air. Any element that could re-enhance itself and obscure the panic of bullets, smoke and the horrifying memory of blazing death. Embracing the whipping rush of the bitter-cold atmosphere remained the welcome tonic. It could gradually replace the sweating fear, abate the dwindling shock of desperate men fighting for survival.

There it was again! Within the sun. He squinted and observed through the shadow his hand created above his goggles. His heart leaped as he gulped. Three wings were falling towards them. The rotating blade was distant but on a course towards their Bristol F2B.

'Enemy dropping from the sun!' Maloney screamed into the voice pipe for all he was worth.

The Bristol F2B engine roared as Lieutenant Adams reacted instantly, briskly pitching the plane upwards and skilfully rolling the entire aircraft as it soared to meet the oncoming threat of the diving Fokker DR1 head-to-head. It all happened so quickly, and Maloney was once again dizzy and disoriented by the rapid upward surge and turn of the aircraft.

'Attack head on is the best course of action!' screamed Adams into the hose funnel. 'Get ready for the blighter as he passes, Maloney.'

'Y-yes, sir,' replied Maloney, trying to steady himself while pulling back the bolt along the right side of the Lewis gun and locking it in readiness. He was out of his disoriented state and turned to glimpse the attacking aircraft over the pilot's shoulder and past the central wing. Then he gave up and peered down past the tail fin again, praying for all he was worth. Why was the instant taking so long? Everything registered in Maloney's mind. He was briefly shaken by the movement of their flimsy-looking elevators and then peered back further beyond the tail fin to the retreating fields of hedgerows and green. Shrinking wisps of cloud lay between them and the distant ground.

'Christ!' he muttered to himself as the engine protested louder and their aircraft continued to climb.

Tearing himself away, Maloney swung the Lewis mount to the plane's port side. The young observer hated having his back to the attack. Why he was expecting the Fokker DR1 to shoot past on the lieutenant's three o'clock, he couldn't say. Was it a spontaneous assumption or perhaps a sixth sense?

'It's von Richthofen!' Adams shouted through the hose funnel.

'Yes, sir,' replied the terrified observer.

'Blast! He's diving at speed, while this old Biff seems to be spluttering and protesting.'

Such words did not inspire confidence. Maloney was sweating with fear again. What was Adams doing? He seemed almost matter of fact. Then the daring pilot's Vickers machine gun beneath the top wing defiantly opened fire.

Pa, pa, pa, pa, pa, pa, pa was the almost impudent sound as his opponent let loose with his twin Spandau guns – ta, ta, ta, ta, ta.

The hissing of projectiles whizzing past ripped off the fabric as one enemy bullet went through the tip of the Bristol F2B's upper wing, just missing the aileron and outer strut.

Maloney opened up with his Lewis gun. The double three-round burst of pa, pa, pa – pa, pa, pa. It instantly got the adrenalin pumping at the vibrant red blur of the Fokker DR1 triplane. The fleeting sight of a red canvas fuselage and black cross inside a white frame rushing past. He slid the Lewis gun mount along to face the rear and followed the resplendent red mass with its contrasting white tail fin. Another short burst was managed – pa, pa, pa. But Maloney knew instantly that his machine-gun fire was unfruitful.

The young observer's mouth dropped open in amazement as the iconic Fokker DR1 triplane seemed to pause mid-air while their own aircraft climbed upwards. He watched the white tail rudder turn left as the entire crimson craft appeared to yaw sideways to port. Almost like stopping dead in mid-air and turning on the spot. Perhaps the upward pitch of their climbing Bristol F2B exaggerated the spectacular sight of the Baron von Richthofen's diabolical air manoeuvre.

Adams was watching in the side mirror. 'Like a naughty schoolboy sliding to a stop along a polished floor, because he's overshot the staircase.'

Maloney gulped in awe. 'Is that the fella all the fuss is about?'

'It certainly is, Maloney. Keep your rump cheeks clenched and hold on to that Lewis for dear life. This will need careful timing, old chap.'

Meanwhile, their Bristol F2B aircraft continued to climb. The majestic side of the red phantom killer was poised in infamous glory, with the black Teutonic cross along its red fuselage and the other smaller decal on the white tail fin. There the dreadful triplane posed while shrinking in its limitless dread. They pitched up and away from the lingering crimson, putting distance between themselves and the dashing air duellist.

Maloney sighed and shook his head in disbelief. There had to be a logical physics explanation within the illusion somewhere. That of the stationary pose of the awesome enemy aircraft. The Red Baron appeared to continue in the magical linger of the red triplane while shrinking in size. There he was, man and machine – the infamous phantom of the sky in all his wicked glory. The red menace's wings wobbled slightly as if they were hovering. What type of trickery was this? Had the German ace turned the engine off and simply stopped? Was it the angle of their own climbing Bristol F2B playing an optical illusion?

'There must be a reason inside that deception,' Maloney berated the Almighty. He was in total disbelief. Perhaps another burst at the still target? Alas, the red tri-winged aeroplane was shrinking ever smaller because of their aircraft's continued climb. Maloney reasoned that he could ill afford to waste bullets.

Then he gasped and felt his skilled enemy's wicked composure sweep over him. The Fokker DR1 majestically fell away into a sideways roll from the appearance of hovering. The quick episode was a dreamlike bubble of slow motion – a prolonged instant or deliberate stall of something akin to. What absolute and terrifying grace. There had to be a reason behind such trickery. How could anyone handle an aircraft like that? Yet this demon air ace could. Maloney found it astonishing. The young observer closed one eye with his mouth open as he looked through the sight of his Lewis, following the arcing line of the red speck, the sideways turn displaying the top wing and the fuselage fairing. The anticipated trajectory of flight as the Red Baron steered his aircraft along in a distant, sweeping curve. A climbing semicircle that would eventually bring the Fokker DR1 around to confront their Bristol F2B from the rear.

'The blighter is approaching from the rear, so he is, sir,' hissed Maloney into his voice pipe, allowing the sight of his Lewis gun to follow the red gnat. A bug that would soon grow in stature as it closed in for the kill.

The anxious observer still refrained from shooting, knowing the distance was now far too great. But he had to keep the Red Baron within the gunsights, even at a distance that was pathetically out of range. His foe was beyond cunning. This anonymity was a ruthless artist. A very hard-hearted one in the air. Such a warrior had to be callous in order to survive. Maloney decided that he must be cold-hearted to prevent the red demon from claiming their aircraft for another of his many kills.

'A man that knows the score,' muttered Maloney. 'If that crimson machine should grow larger within the sight…'

Lieutenant Adams' voice came through the Gosport headset. 'He's not finished yet, Maloney. That blighter is circling for another attack.'

'I'm ready for him, sir.' Maloney peered through his goggles.

He took another deep breath. He sounded much more confident than he felt. He gasped before running his tongue along his chapped lips. For a moment, the Fokker DR1 was a big red mass. How on earth had his machine-gun burst missed his target? The whole thing about air-to-air combat was so much more difficult than anyone might imagine. Judging the firing distance ahead of the flight path. But an attack from the aircraft's rear did keep the target area a little more defined, he reasoned to himself. There had to be a chance if the Red Baron attacked from the rear.

'Sir, did the Baron just stop the engine? Or is that some sort of trick?' Maloney called into his voice funnel, watching the red speck appear on the port flank. A manoeuvre for a new attack.

'I'm not sure if the Baron's engine stopped or if it was a trick or function the blighter is aware of. Considering his yaw of the aircraft and our pitch adding to the grand illusion, I assume the latter. That was quite an introduction for you, Maloney.'

'Well, I'm not feeling too privileged by the performance now, sir,' Maloney joked nervously.

Adams hollered, 'I understand perfectly, old boy. This ace is full of tricks. I think he's a bit of a show-off, but no one seems to be able to tell him. Stay alert, Maloney. Von Richthofen will climb and circle for another approach. Be ready for an attack from the rear. This next one will probably be down to you to see off.'

'Yes, sir. Did that red thing swerve to the side or was it us, when we passed each other, sir?' shouted Maloney.

Adams' voice screamed back along the funnel, 'A bit of both, old boy. Keep your sights on the tricky blighter and don't spend too much time admiring him. Look for something you can exploit. I'm going to try Captain Polden's advice and drop down low when we reach the vicinity of the Ozzie trenches. We'll need to fight off other attacks to get a chance of getting there. Ozzie ground fire is dashed rude and rather fierce, according to our late Captain Polden – God rest his soul. Right now, that's our best option.'

'Well now, sir, I'll be of the opinion that the good old Ozzie can be as rude as he likes with this fella. Oh, sweet Lord, I think he's coming in for another pop at us, so he is, sir.'

Adams chuckled. 'That's the spirit, Maloney.'

The buzz of the Red Baron's engine whirred as Maloney watched the triplane's progressive climb.

'The Baron is moving higher than we are, sir.'

Then he wobbled forward and watched with further alarm. The retreating ground came into view once again. Lieutenant Adams pitched their Biff further up too. He pitched up to maximum height before engaging the Fokker DR1. Again, Maloney was disbelieving and aghast at how daring Adams was. He gulped, realising the lieutenant was trying to give the famous ace a full-on dogfight with no holding back on anyone's part. No quarters asked, none given.

'Prepare to open up on the fellow, Mahoney. Give our Red Baron everything you can muster. Aim and take short bursts. Don't blaze away unless you have the target close. And he will come in close.

Mark my words he will. He must in order shoot us down.'

'Yes, sir,' Mahoney answered. His stomach churned. He wanted the red devil to attack. Get it over with. Let the guns open up. Maloney's fear was clouded by anger and determination. He gritted his teeth and followed the ascending red triplane in his gun-sights.

The enemy Fokker DR1 twisted and turned as the Bristol F2B responded accordingly. Each aircraft circled like giant birds of prey and their engines droned like agitated wasps. Then came a skilled twisting full turnover of the lighter and sleeker Fokker DR1. An acrobatic roll across the divide of the circling aircraft. The crimson machine neatly dropped into a killing position behind their Biff's tail fin some three hundred yards off. Maloney stared open-mouthed as the triplane gently rolled from side to side. It was still some way off, but the intention was very clear. Maloney could clearly see the Baron von Richthofen. The goggles and the leather flying helmet. A windswept scarf danced in the breeze. His glittering medal hung beneath his exposed tunic's collar. The enigma of the man was already moving his hands between his twin Spandau machine guns. Then he started priming them in readiness as he looked sternly over the front of his cockpit. Readying to unleash synchronised .312 bullets through the rotating propeller blades.

'The Hun is right behind us and closing in, sir,' Mahoney yelled, re-checking the bolt of his Lewis gun remained locked in readiness.

Lieutenant Adams abruptly rolled the Bristol F2B sharply to port. An unexpected move that caught the pursuing Red Baron by surprise. Maloney gritted his teeth and grinned as he watched the enemy pilot's head movement. The deadly air ace was clearly taken aback. The enemy aircraft's engines responded with an angry roar and the Fokker DR1 accelerated as it tried to follow Adams' line of flight. Maloney put his eye to the rear sight of his Lewis and levelled it with the front sight of the barrel just as the red blur through rotating propellers smothered the line of fire.

Immediately, instinct kicked in and Maloney squeezed the trigger – pa, pa – pa, pa, pa, pa. He saw a spark on the wheel strut as the Fokker DR1 veered to the starboard and away from their own plane's trajectory. The enemy engine howled as it fell, rolling away from the brief fray.

'I hit something!' screamed Maloney excitedly. 'I saw sparks, sir.'

'Where?' Adams screamed back excitedly.

'One of the wheel struts, I think.'

'Oh!' replied the pilot. He was obviously disappointed after having his hopes built up. 'Don't count on that as a crippling shot, Maloney. Don't take your eyes off him. Richthofen will be back. He wants us as another chalked-up kill.'

'Yes, sir,' Maloney replied as he watched the red triplane level out and circle around. After that, it began to climb again. The distant engine howled angrily as the aircraft fervently ascended into the sky behind them. To Maloney's astonishment, Lieutenant Adams called out through the hose.

'Let's climb too. We must match his aggression with our own. Run and he'll have us. Let's meet our prize Hun head on.'

Maloney gulped and scolded the move in his petrified thoughts. *Oh my God! What's the lieutenant doing?*

Instantly, the Bristol F2B roared angrily as it pitched upwards too. Both aircraft seemed to find a new level area of battle where the duel might continue. Once again, the circling began. A spiralling descent as each aircraft chased their opponent's twisting and meandering tail. The Fokker DR1 performed better as it suddenly rolled again, circling over the divide to fall in closer behind. Yet Lieutenant Adams gave the Red Baron no time to settle as he did the same rolling turn. Maloney became disoriented and petrified. The turning sky and then the turning ground. Everything made him nauseous with fear.

'Sorry about that, Maloney, but get your wits back as quick as you can, lad. Richthofen will fall in behind us again soon. He'll not fall for that a second time. When he adapts again, he'll come as close as possible before letting off a burst. You must beat him to it. Do you think you can do that, Maloney?'

'Yes, sir. I think I can do that,' replied Maloney nervously.

At that very moment, the crimson pursuer fell in behind their plane's vertical fin once again. Maloney had already pulled the bolt back and locked it in readiness. The rear sight aligned with the front as the weaving Fokker DR1 tried to present a difficult target. Maloney bit his lips, wanting to find his own killing shot. A fledgling sparrow against a hawk.

The young observer held his breath and moved the Lewis gun on its swivel. A brief sight of crimson and a quick squeeze – pa, pa, pa. Another red blur and another pa, pa, pa, pa.

Suddenly, the flashes came from the Red Baron's plane as his twin Spandau machine guns spat out a wicked response – ta, ta, ta, ta, ta.

Adams turned the Bristol F2B sharply to the left at precisely that moment having just watched the scene before him through the rear-view mirror. All enemy .312 bullets whizzed past without striking. The engine screamed in protest as Maloney gripped the rim of his observer cockpit knowing he was heading into another somersaulting roll. God, he hoped the straps would hold firm. Once again, the nausea of twisting blue sky and distant, far away earth turning while he tried to control his terrified wits. The young observer was certain these moves were not part of standard practice, and he was beginning to realise that Lieutenant Adams was a wild card – a chancer all the way. He couldn't believe his eyes as the Bristol F2B slowly dropped upright and levelled out behind the Fokker DR1. A glorious but brief uplifting moment as Adams let loose with his Vickers machine gun – pa, pa, pa, pa, pa. The moment was lost and so was von Richthofen as he counter-moved with another flanking roll away from the pursuit. The pilot had astonishing skill and panache.

'How the blooming heck did he do that?' shouted Maloney.

'He's bloody good. We're not out of the woods yet, Maloney. Get back to that gun and keep the Hun in sight. Watch for a drop or upsurge behind the vertical fin.'

As Adams alerted Maloney to the move, the Red Baron's aircraft suddenly dropped into view. The distance was too great to shoot either aircraft.

Suddenly, Adams went into a twisting dive, the Fokker DR1 falling in hot pursuit. Maloney watched the tail fin and rudder move on either side of the screaming red chaser. The aircraft matched the moves as it neared, engines screaming in protest while tearing through the air. Maloney was jostling with the jumping sights, trying to match them against the chasing crimson machine that was dancing in and out of the gun-sights.

He flinched at the flashes of the twin Spandau machine guns, expecting to see or feel the projectiles impact. There was no sound of bullets whizzing past or hitting them. Maloney still refrained from shooting. Was the ace trying to trick him into returning fire at such a distance? Was the Baron trying to make him deplete his magazine before killing him? Maloney's mind raced. Was this part of the crimson ace's acquired knowledge?

The planes were still diving, the engines still screaming when Maloney stealthily grabbed the smaller forty-seven-round drum magazine. Why not try the ploy? Gingerly, he pulled it from a bracket mounted inside his observer's cockpit. The very magazine Cooper and Norris had recommended that he take for good luck. The one with no rounds left inside. Through the wind-rush, he could clearly make out the pursuing red triplane. He even noticed the twinkle of the Pour le Mérite on the front of Baron von Richthofen's collar – even glimpsing the tiny blue strips. Yet the ace still needed to get closer and steadier instead of bouncing about behind in the ripping turbulence of their Bristol F2B.

Maloney raised himself, offering his opponent a full view of an inexperienced rear gunner. He acted as if he were trying to change the drum. Allowing the ace to see as he leaned forward and over the Lewis gun front, pretending to wrestle with the magazine. A complete show of ineptitude for the enemy Baron who would be watching and making ready for his closing attack. As the young observer pretended to wrestle with the drum magazine, he feigned falling back for the chasing enemy aircraft, holding aloft the pan magazine and playing the buffoon. Showing the predator what the yearning combatant of experience might want to see. He even stage-managed another stagger before finally and deliberately dropping the drum magazine over the side for the enemy ace to clearly see. It was the bait and Maloney knew the Red Baron had taken it. The engine of the Fokker DR1 whirred with increased glee. The Baron charged without further hesitation. The leather-covered head, the black goggles, the grinning face with the gold Pour le Mérite at the throat. The whole vision – coming closer for the kill. Maloney expected the spread of machine-gun fire at any moment.

Lieutenant Adams screamed incoherently through the Gosport's earmuffs. This didn't matter. Maloney was in his own zone and ignored both pilots. His original drum magazine was still in place with a substantial number of .303 rounds. He had dropped the useless and empty mag to encourage the now growing image of the whirling propeller, a leather-capped head with black goggles and gritting teeth.

'Will you not come for your booby prize, Mr Baron?' whispered Maloney teasingly as the triplane's screaming engine reached its crescendo. He imagined that his enemy might be listening and his blood rushed as the Fokker DR1 drew nearer.

Everything became sharp and clear within the dreamlike moments that followed. For Maloney, his senses slowed down. Everything was carried out in a slow, drawn-out split second of time. As a lifetime might flash through a doomed person's mind, so did the moments of the following action. Maloney swiftly grabbed the left side of the bar mount and grasped the lower gun handle with his forefinger on the trigger. Teeth gritted, he gently squeezed as his Lewis gun spat out defiantly.

The first rapid shot started with the usual pa – the sound of the discharged shell and the casing springing out of the side. The slow motion played out in the small instant of time as his vision took the surreal moments in.

Pa…

The second round as he watched the Baron's red menace approach.

Pa...

The third of the rapid shots showed Maloney the gratifying change in his foe's ill-deserved confidence. The leather-capped head with earflaps, the black goggles and the open mouth as a spark appeared on the upper central wing just above and before the pilot's shocked face. The natural flinch of the head...

Pa...

The following fourth round smashed against the front scarlet strut that came out of the engine fuselage at a thirty-degree angle to connect with the underneath of the top wing. The contrast of the tiny thin blue strips within the pilot's golden Pour le Mérite.

Pa...

The fifth and final shot of the first five-round burst as the crimson machine became an evasive blur and vanished sideways from Maloney's gunsights. He cussed and quickly swung the gun mount around to point the Lewis down, knowing that two of his shots had definitely struck. The acting observer gritted his teeth with vicious joy. His faithful Lewis gun's second and third burst sang out – pa, pa, pa, pa. Pa, pa, pa, pa. His gun's barrel tried to follow the flight path of the evading triplane. He watched another two strikes. One into the red canvas fuselage fairing and the other hitting the upper white tail fin with its black cross.

Each strike was merely superficial. Yet Maloney reasoned it might give the infamous Red Baron something to think about. The thought was short-lived. The red Fokker DR1 continued to arc out-wards and away at a lowering altitude. The engine gradually moved away, then changed pitch, circling around the Bristol F2B once again. An angry little red hornet getting ready to continue attacking – game for the kill.

'Hits on the strut, the central wing, the fuselage and the fin, sir. No real damage, but enough to make the ace take evasive action.'

'Dashed well done, Maloney. Keep a watch. I think you might have the old boy's gander up.' Adams grinned through his clenched teeth and at the pain of his wounded arm.

Lieutenant Adams was correct concerning the Red Baron's pride. The red triplane was jostling about but clearly levelling up for another attack. It seemed to level behind for a moment and then con-tinue further around before arcing sharply to their starboard flank.

'I think he's coming in on the starboard flank this time, sir,' Maloney yelled into his voice pipe.

'Let's get ready to drop. We're getting close to the Ozzie front-line section,' Adams replied, want-ing to let the Baron make his run before going into his dive. 'This one will need careful timing,' he called through Maloney's earmuffs.

'Here he comes, sir!' Maloney twisted the Lewis mount about to face the incoming side attack. There was no time to get a fix on the red triplane. The whole target fell away from his gun-sights as Adams took the Bristol F2B into a sharp port-side roll and drop. He heard the duel ta, ta, ta, ta of the Red Baron's Spandau guns. Saw a couple of hits along their side fuselage and felt the whizz of a projectile just missing him.

Adams cursed out in pain, while Maloney saw the underneath of the Baron's plane as the red mass shot past and veered majestically away from his gun-sights. In the same vein, the observer let loose with another spread. Pa, pa, pa, pa. No new strikes but he did see the previous punctures. He had time to notice the black cross emblem within the white square section of canvas as their own turning biplane twisted the ace from his view. Twirling sky and disorientation for a few seconds before gathering his jumbled wits again. Now Maloney could look at Lieutenant Adams. He called into his voice funnel and leaned backwards towards the pilot. 'Are you alright, sir?'

'I think so,' said Adams with a gasp. 'This dashed shoulder is giving me some serious gip, old chap. Hold on tight. We're dropping towards the Ozzie lines down there and I've a feeling you may have hurt Richthofen's pride a little too much. That means he might come back for another helping.

Dashed greedy these Hun aces. Maybe he'll chase us down?'

Maloney looked up over the tail fin and saw that the distant red Fokker DR1 was doing just that. Circling for a last chance of a kill. Another notch for the Red Baron's tally.

'You're right, so you are, sir. If the old red devil isn't about to dive down back at us.'

The rumbling engine of the Fokker DR1 screamed as the red dot got larger and the pitch of the engine grew louder.

This time Maloney quickly pulled up a fresh ninety-seven-round drum magazine from the bracket. He took off the old drum and firmly slid and clicked the replacement in place. He stacked the used drum back in the rack while their Bristol F2B engine screamed its diving descent. Maloney checked the feed into the gun barrel – not wanting a double feed situation in the middle of a new shoot-out. Even glancing at the air coolant vents for further reassurance. All seemed in order as the enemy triplane continued to scream down for a fresh encounter.

'Here he comes, sir!' Maloney yelled.

The Bristol F2B continued to dive – the Fokker DR1 followed – no more beautiful patchwork of fields, just the ugly cratered earth rising to meet them. Maloney stared up at their would-be nemesis, gaining at an alarming speed. He swivelled the Lewis gun in place and aimed – fired a short burst, but the jostling target was still too distant. Suddenly Maloney fell forward as their Bristol sharply levelled and then pitched slightly upwards. The Red Baron's red Fokker triplane shot past them again as bullets hissed harmlessly by.

Suddenly, their plucky Biff levelled at around two thousand feet and raced over no man's land towards their own positions. Maloney prayed that the Australian trenches would recognise them as the enemy trench had not started firing yet but that might change at any moment.

'He's gone up and is circling for one more, Maloney,' called Adams, clearly in distress from his wounded shoulder. 'Give him everything and sod the wasted bullets, old chap.'

'Yes, sir,' screamed Maloney as he saw then heard the whine of the Fokker DR1 engine screaming a path towards them. He raised the Lewis gun to meet the diving red machine. He opened up far too early, but decided to let every bullet spit. Let the guns jam – let them overheat – what did it matter? With his teeth gritting, the Lewis spat defiantly – pa, pa, pa, pa, pa, pa, pa, pa, pa, pa, pa...

Then he saw the fire flashes of the twin Spandau machine guns firing through the propellers. Was the Baron von Richthofen too far away as well?

Suddenly, the red triplane was gone. Obscured by a wall of anti-aircraft flak, splattering smoke and shrapnel between them and the Red Baron's Fokker DR1 triplane. Was the crimson phantom gone? He was supposed to be unyielding.

Their glorious small Biff dropped steeply to under one thousand feet as they approached the Australian lines. Enemy guns from the trenches to the rear opened up.

'That was Ozzie flak, Maloney,' Adams yelled in pain. 'We've gone and blooming done it, old chap.' As they flew low over the lines, Maloney could hear and see the cheering Australian soldiers in the trench works. It was a sight for sore eyes. The applause was very encouraging indeed. He chanced a look up into the sky and saw the retreating red speck of the Red Baron's aircraft returning home to fly another day.

Maloney muttered with dread, 'He who turns and runs away, lives to fight another day. The Red Baron is still with us, sir. Though not anymore for this day.'

Their Biff's engine suddenly spluttered as the sound of something snapping pinged beneath the engine cowling. A thin line of light grey smoke streamed from the port exhaust manifold. Maloney jumped and called out, 'What the hell was that, sir?'

The cheering of the Australian front-line soldiers died away as their smoking aircraft flew into their own territory. The engine coughed and spluttered, but doggedly continued on. The thin stream of smoke was still pouring along the port side from the exhaust manifold. For the first time, Maloney could see one of the bullet strikes on the grey engine casing.

'Was that from ground fire coming from the enemy trenches as we crossed our lines?' Lieutenant Adams asked.

'I never heard any of the bullets strike, sir.' Maloney was perplexed. 'Perhaps the Baron scored a hit without us realising it?'

'I never noticed it at the time,' Adams responded. 'Perhaps when we were diving to evade and the engines were screaming. Easily could have drowned out the sound of a strike.'

'We're still streaming smoke, sir,' called Maloney nervously.

'I know, old chap,' Adams grumbled through his pain. 'I'm staying low and avoiding the clusters of trees. I've shut off the Jones valve and I think I can get this old Biff back home. But just in case we need to chance it and ditch, I'm picking the nice big fields to fly over at a low level. And I do mean nice bloody big fields with as few tree clusters as possible. Landing and rolling into trees is often not too good. It's about eight miles to our airfield. Therefore, we might as well give it a go via the open meadows.'

'Well, I think I like the sound of that, sir. Can you hold out that long? I'm not talking about the Biff, sir. I mean, will you be needing help?'

'Thank you for asking, old chap, but I think I can hold in here.' Adams was being cheerfully sarcastic. 'On another note, you did blooming well back there. We may be able to boast that we took on the Red Baron and lived to tell the tale. You even ripped the blighter's canvas.'

'I blooming well hope so, sir. Though gratitude must go to those Ozzies back there.' Maloney laughed as he decided they must surely make it now. He looked down nervously at the smoke stream billowing out of the exhaust pipe along the side fuselage past their respective cockpits and leaving a thin trail stretching back to the front. Below, the meadows and trees passed them by. They were edging ever closer to the airfield and home.

'The late Captain Polden swore to the fact that those Ozzie chaps are hoping to have a go at the Red Baron from the ground. Who knows, maybe one day. He almost ran into them this time and Captain Polden said he almost did when chasing him too.'

'Well, I'm glad we made it this far, sir. I hope we can do the whole thing, that's for sure.'

'One birthday you'll never forget in a hurry – what! I would imagine you might think back to this birthday every time you get a year older.' Adams chuckled, wincing from his shoulder wound and wrestling with the stick's circular grip. It was still nerve-wracking but less so than the duel they'd been through.

Maloney kept listening to the inner workings of the plane and then added, 'Well, there's reason for optimism despite the stuttering noise in this troubled Falcon III engine. I think she'll hold. The bounce when we land might be a little tricky, sir. I don't think this old girl is going to like it much.'

Both men laughed nervously while still checking the skies. It didn't pay to be over-confident, even inside one's own lines. After a time, they could see their airfield in the distance. Adams called out in delight, 'There she is, old chap.'

The smoke trail that their Bristol F2B was leaving must have alerted the personnel. Aircrew and vehicles were fanning out to meet them. Adams gently lowered the aircraft towards the grass runway. There was another bang from within the engine casing. The billowing black smoke became a little thicker, and the trailing plume was suddenly darker.

'Hold on, old chap,' hissed Adams as their aircraft lowered unsteadily and a little quicker than each man felt comfortable with. The entire plane shook violently as the front of the aircraft flared a little too high. The wheels smashed down heavily and bounced the entire Bristol F2B. The two hundred and seventy-five h.p. engine bent the axels instantly and the light airframe had parts snapping here and upon the canvas cover. The entire broken vehicle returned on an already bent axel. The engine mounts snapped on the second slam down. Maloney was thrown off his seat by the impact, and smashed his shoulder against the Lewis gun mounts before his harness restraints stopped him from going further. His collarbone snapped, and he screamed in pain, bouncing backwards into his wicker seat. His leg caught in a part of the magazine stacking rails and he let out a second scream of agony as his shin bone cracked. Two bone breaks in almost an instant.

The entire front of the plane collapsed into the grass upon the broken wheel axle and the tail shot upright and threatened to turn completely over. It lingered at ninety degrees for a moment before slamming back down upon its shattered under-belly.

Maloney had blacked out momentarily. It was mere moments when he woke to further excruciating pain. There were flames and black smoke about him – heat and the noise of shouting rescuers. He tried to stand and winced again – aware that his harness held him inside. Reflex actions were working through the severe trauma of his broken collarbone and shattered shin. He reached down and tried to unclip himself with his good arm. Hands were reaching over the cockpit and cutting the harness straps. More hands pulling him as he screamed. His leg was still caught in the magazine rack.

'Gently, gently,' called the voice of a red cross man.

'His foot is caught in the mag rack,' called another as more figures leaned into the cockpit. Many hands carefully lifted his lower leg free of the restraining container. Maloney winced and groaned at the discomfort but knew time was of the essence as the burning grew more intense. Then, through the discomfort, he was borne out of the burning Bristol F2B and taken across the wet grass, aware of another throng of personnel carrying Lieutenant Adams across the turf as well.

Then came the boom as their aircraft erupted in flames. The leaking fuel had ignited into an orange ball of flames that rolled around the two cockpits where he and the lieutenant had been moments earlier. Within seconds, the canvas body was burning away fiercely, and more thick black smoke climbed into the air.

'Dermot,' came the voice of Tibby. The new recruit of his hangar's flight mechanic team. He was among the medical staff and fire fighters. Norris and Cooper were there too while medical orderlies were putting down a stretcher.

'Is Lieutenant Adams alright? Has he been hit?' Maloney asked.

'He's been pulled out too,' replied Norris. 'The medical bloke who helped pull you out is with him. I heard tell that he'll be alright. The lieutenant is asking after you. The orderly is assuring him that you'll be alright, and says you have a broken collarbone and a broken shin.'

'Yes, Norris.' Maloney chuckled through his discomfort. 'Trust me, fella – I know.'

'We had a few eats and drinks ready for your twentieth,' added Cooper.

'We'll have to eat the birthday cake and drink a beer for you, Dermot,' added Tibbit light-heartedly. 'I'm so pleased you got back. That has to be one hell of a birthday to remember.'

Maloney looked up and smiled. 'Don't learn too many useful things, Tibby. Trust me, fella. You don't want them sending you up there. I don't care if I never get in another kite as long as I live.'

'Whoever got onto you, he only got the plane eventually. You lived to tell the tale,' said Tibbit.

Maloney reached up and gripped Tibbit's shoulder. 'We had a blooming good old shoot-out with von Richthofen, Tibby, that's for sure. He didn't see this crash, so I doubt it's a confirmed kill. By that, I mean he can't claim it. Not as confirmed.'

Cooper frowned as he looked at the burning wreckage of the Bristol F2B. 'That old girl got you and the lieutenant home. At a cost to the old kite you're an unconfirmed kill of the Red Baron. Two of you live to tell the tale.'

Norris raised his eyebrows humorously. 'On the plus side, Dermot – you've got yourself a long lie-in. Collarbones and shin bones are tricky. They take time to repair.'

'The longer the better.' Maloney groaned amid the crackle of flames devouring the Bristol F2B. The cremation of a plane that served them well.

RONNIE IN AWE OF HIS GREAT

GRANDAD – APRIL 5TH, 1980

'So, you were shot down by the Red Baron? This little man in this aircraft?' Ronnie was staring at his red plastic World War One Fokker DR1 model that Pop was holding. All painted red with black cross decals. 'You actually fought against that plane?'

Pop smiled and replied in his Irish accent, 'I certainly did, young fella. And it's something that never leaves me.' He reached over and gave him back his plastic model.

'My word, Pop,' added Philip. 'That is quite a story.'

'But a true one nonetheless, Philip. I can remember it as though it were yesterday. And always on my birthday.'

Ronnie moved to the side of the armchair and turned the model around before Pop's gaze.

The old man nodded. 'I know I'm repeating myself, but the figure in the cockpit was definitely wearing black goggles, that's for sure, young Ronnie. And just in front of his collar, I can still remember that striking thin blue cross over a glittering circular gold background. I'll never forget that. You might want to ask yer dad if he could get that put on the figure. You'll need a very thin-haired brush, that's for sure.'

'I can do that, Pop,' Philip said as he approached the mantelpiece and looked at the birthday cards. 'I have a small enough model brush in the garden shed. I never thought about that. I also have goggles and a Blue Max medal.'

Ronnie was full of excitement and admiration. 'Pop would know. He has seen this plane, Dad. Back in the first war and on his twentieth birthday. That's why he gets Tibby's letter from New Zealand on his birthday. Isn't it, Pop?'

'This is so, young Ronnie.' Pop smiled down at the boy.

Philip grinned in the way an adult does when a young boy is being told a yarn by an old great grandad. But then his smile gradually faded as he noted the serious look in Pop's eyes.

'I thought you were just a mechanic, Pop.' Philip's look became perplexed. 'I never realised you did these other things.'

'I was an air mechanic, Philip. A happy one for most of the time, except for that one occasion when I was seconded to go up as an acting observer. And on that one occurrence I encountered the Red Baron while returning from our mission. He inflicted damage upon our aircraft before being driven off by Australian ground fire as we soared over our lines. Of that, Lieutenant Adams and I were pretty sure.'

'Yes, I see what you mean, Pop,' said Philip, thinking about the story he had heard.

Pop laughed. 'For a while, Lieutenant Adams and I marvelled at our survival of being an uncon-firmed Red Baron kill. If the ace knew, he could have claimed our Biff as a confirmed kill. Some of his confirmed kills had aircrew that survived to tell the tale. Though not very many. We were lucky to have him driven off.'

'By Australian soldiers!' added Ronnie excitedly.

Philip frowned as he sat in the armchair opposite Pop and repeated his amazement of the tale. 'I never knew you actually went up in a plane. The whole story is extraordinary.'

'My first and only time,' Pop replied. 'My pilot, Lieutenant Adams, and I went on to see out the war to its end.'

Philip sighed. 'So when you say unconfirmed kill, you mean the Red Baron didn't get the credit for it?'

'No, he did not. The old ace didn't know of our crash. He was seen off by the Ozzie ground fire before we got back to our airfield and crashed during the landing.'

'I heard he was shot down by a Canadian pilot,' added Philip, intrigued by what Pop was saying.

'A few weeks later, the Red Baron met his end and was killed on those very Australian lines. He finally flew low over those trenches, and I heard Australian soldiers were firing away at him from every direction. The Baron chased a Canadian pilot with another chasing him. I was told all of this when I got out of the hospital a few months later.'

'Where did the Red Baron crash?' asked little Ronnie.

'I was told that he simply landed the plane in a field on our side of the lines. His plane's undercarriage collapsed during landing. When Australian soldiers got to the plane, the Baron was sitting in the cockpit dead. A bullet in his chest. No one knows for sure who killed the ace. The air force reckon it was their Canadian lad, while the Ozzies say it was one of their soldiers. No one can say for sure.'

'What happened when you were released from hospital and ready to go back?' Philip was enthralled. Pop was telling a very true story.

'I was out for almost three months. And even when I did return, I was on light duties. I found Cooper and Norris doing what they always did. Tibby was with them and wise to the ways of the Bristol F2B by this time. We had two new planes and two new aircrews – pilots and observers for each. Major Laws had been moved upwards and away. The new overseeing officer that did the rounds of the airfields never asked or requested me in an acting observer role again. I must say I was grateful for that and didn't feel the need to remind anyone.'

'So, you remained an air mechanic?' Philip was more interested than his son Ronnie.

'That I did, for the last four months or so of the war. I kept a low profile and from that day to the armistice. I never knew why they left me alone, but I was sure glad they did.'

'Did you see Lieutenant Adams again?' asked Ronnie.

'I did not, Ronnie. But I did hear of him. He was invalided out of flying but remained in the RAF doing other duties at the training grounds. He continued to do this even after the war ended. And I wouldn't be at all surprised if he was in that second war as some sort of high-ranking pen-pusher. He was a fine man and I hope he lived a good life. I heard he passed away back in 1974 – God rest his soul.'

'What of Cooper, Norris and Tibby?' Ronnie grinned. He liked stories with happy endings.

'Cooper and Norris went their own way after the war. I lost touch with them. Tibby, on the other hand, became a good friend in those final months of the war. He emigrated to New Zealand back in 1923, but he has always stayed in touch on my birthday. He lives in a place called Nelson. I have never failed to get a letter from him just before the day of my birthday. I always leave it unopened until the very day of my birthday. Never before and only on my birthday. Then I always reply to him on the evening of my birthday.' Pop smiled as he picked up the blue airmail letter.

'Is that Tibby's letter?' asked Ronnie.

'It is, young fella. Should I read it out to you?'

'Yes, please,' replied Ronnie.

'I think that would be a splendid thing,' added Philip. There was a feeling of warmth and delight as Pop opened his airmail letter from his old air force friend from World War One. A friend he had met on his twentieth birthday sixty-two years to the day.

Printed in Great Britain
by Amazon

40158294R00136